W9-DIJ-012

RESCUED BY HIS
CHRISTMAS ANGEL

RESCUED BY HIS CHRISTMAS ANGEL

BY

CARA COLTER

MILLS & BOON

First published in Great Britain 2010
Large Print edition 2011
Harlequin Mills & Boon Limited,
Eton House, 18-24 Paradise Road,
Richmond, Surrey TW9 1SR

ISBN: 978 0 263 22191 6

Harlequin Mills & Boon policy is to use papers that are natural, renewable and recyclable products and made from wood grown in sustainable forests. The logging and manufacturing process conform to the legal environmental regulations of the country of origin.

Printed and bound in Great Britain
by CPI Antony Rowe, Chippenham, Wiltshire

To Lynne and Larry Cormack
with heartfelt gratitude
for twenty-five years of friendship

CHAPTER ONE

TEARS. BOOKS THROWN. And pencils. Breakage. Name-calling. Screaming. Hair-pulling. It was like a scene from a bad marriage or the kind of drama that a reality television show *adored,* rife with mayhem, conflicts, conspiracies.

But it wasn't a bad marriage, or bad TV.

It was Morgan McGuire's life, and it didn't help one bit that each of the perpetrators in today's drama had been under four feet tall. The day had culminated with a twenty-one-child "dog pile on the rabbit."

It was the kind of day they had failed to prepare her for at teacher's college, Morgan, first-year first-grade teacher, thought mournfully.

And somehow, fair or not, in her mind, it was all *his* fault.

Nate Hathoway, father of Cecilia Hathoway, the

child who had been at the very center of every single kerfuffle today, including being the rabbit in that unfortunate dog pile.

Now, Morgan McGuire paused and stared at the sign in front of her. Hathoway's Forge. Her heart was beating hard, and it wasn't just from the walk from school, either.

Don't do it, her fellow teacher Mary Beth Adams had said when Morgan had asked her at lunch if she thought she should go beard the lion in his den.

Or the devil at his fire, as the case might be.

"But he's ignoring my notes. He hasn't signed the permission slip for Cecilia—"

"Cecilia?"

Morgan sighed. "Ace. Her real name's Cecilia. I think she needs something feminine in her life, including her name. That was what the first fight this morning was about. Her hairstyle."

Not that the haircut was that new, but today there had been a very unusual new styling for the haircut. How could *he* have let her out of the house looking like that?

"And then," Morgan continued, "one of the kids overheard me ask her about the permission slip to be in *The Christmas Angel*. She didn't have it."

The production of *The Christmas Angel* was descending on Canterbury, Connecticut.

The town had been chosen by the reclusive, aging troubadour Wesley Wellhaven for his second annual Christmas extravaganza.

The fact that Mr. Wellhaven would be using local children—the first graders would be his backup choir if Cecilia managed to get her permission slip signed—had whipped the children into a frenzy of excitement and dramatic ambition.

"Morgan, rehearsals are starting next week! Mrs. Wellhaven is arriving to supervise the choir!" Mary Beth said this urgently, as if the fact could have somehow bypassed her fellow teacher.

"I know. And I already told the class that we are all doing it, or none of us is doing it."

"That was foolish," Mary Beth said. "Can't

Ace Hathoway just sit in the hall and read a book while the rest of the children rehearse?"

"No!" Morgan was aghast at the suggestion. But meanwhile, poor Cecilia was being seen as the class villain because she was the only one with no permission slip. "If I don't talk to him, Cecilia is going to continue to suffer."

Mary Beth shook her head. "Just let her sit in the hall."

"It's not just the permission slip. I have to address some other issues."

"You know that expression about going where angels fear to tread? That would be particularly true of Hathoway's Forge. Nate wasn't Mr. Sunshine and Light before his wife died. Now…" Mary Beth's voice trailed away and then she continued. "It's not entirely Nate's fault, anyway. Kids always get high-strung around Christmas. It's hitting early because of all the hoopla around the whole *Christmas Angel* thing."

Naturally, Morgan had chosen to ignore Mary Beth's well-meaning advice about going to visit Nate Hathoway.

Now, taking a deep breath, she turned off the pavement and up the winding gravel driveway, lined by trees, now nearly naked of leaves. The leaves, yellow and orange, crunched under her feet, sending up clouds of tart aroma.

Morgan came to a white house, cozy and cottagelike, amongst a grove of trees. It was evident to her that while once it had been well loved, now it looked faintly neglected. The flower beds had not grown flowers this year, but weeds, now depressingly dead. Indigo paint, that once must have looked lively and lovely against the white, was peeling from the shutters, the window trim and the front door that was set deep under a curved arch.

Despite the fact light was leeching from the late-afternoon autumn air, there were no lights on in the house.

Morgan knew Cecilia was at the after-school program.

The road continued on to a building beyond the house. It dwarfed the house, a turn-of-the-century stone barn, but a chimney belched smoke, and light poured out the high upper windows. Morgan realized it was the forge.

She drew nearer to it. A deep, solid door, under a curved arch that mirrored the one on the house, had a sign on it.

Go Away.

That was the kind of unfriendly message, when posted on a door, that one should probably pay strict attention to.

But Morgan hadn't come this far to go away. She drew a deep breath, stepped forward and knocked on the door. And was ignored.

She was absolutely determined she was not going to be ignored by this man anymore! She knocked again, and then, when there was no answer, turned the handle and stepped in.

She was not sure what she expected: smoke, darkness, fire, but the cavernous room was large and bright. What was left of the day's natural light was flowing in windows high up the walls, supplemented by huge shop lights.

In a glance she saw whiskey-barrel bins close to the door full of black wrought iron fireplace pokers and ash shovels, an army of coat holders, stacks of pot racks. Under different circumstances, she would have looked at the wares with great interest.

Nate Hathoway, she had learned since coming to Canterbury, had a reputation as one of the finest artistic blacksmiths in the world.

But today, her gaze went across the heated room to where a fire burned in a great hearth, a man in front of it.

His back was to her, and even though Morgan suspected he had heard her knock, and even heard her enter, he did not turn.

From the back, he was a breathtaking specimen. Dark brown hair, thick and shiny, scraped where a leather apron was looped around his neck over a denim shirt. His shoulders were huge and wide, tapering perfectly down to a narrow waist, where the apron was tied. Faded jeans rode low on nonexistent hips, hugged the slight swell of a perfect masculine butt.

Even though his name was whispered with a kind of reverence by every single female Morgan

had encountered in Canterbury, she felt unpre-
pared for the pure *presence* of him, for that
masculine *something* that filled the air around
him.

She felt as if the air was being sucked from her
lungs and she debated just leaving quietly before
he turned.

Then she chided herself for such a weak
thought. She was here for the good of a six-year-
old child who needed her intervention.

And she was *so* over being swayed by the attractions of men. A bitter breakup with her own
fiancé after she'd had the audacity to consider the
job—her own career—in Canterbury still stung.
Karl had been astonished that she would consider
the low-paid teaching position in the tiny town,
then openly annoyed that his own high-powered
career didn't come first. For both of them.

Morgan was making a new start here. No more
stars in her eyes, no more romantic notions.

Her mother, whom Morgan had thought liked
Karl, had actually breathed a sigh of relief at
Morgan's breakup news.

Darling, I do wish you'd quit looking for a father figure. It makes me feel so guilty.

Not guilty enough, however, to postpone her vacation to Thailand so they could spend Christmas together. In lieu of sympathy over her daughter's failed engagement her mother had given her a book.

It was called *Bliss: The Extraordinary Joy of Being a Single Woman.*

Surprisingly, given that she had initially resented the book being given to her in the place of some parental direction about how to handle a breakup, Morgan found she was thoroughly enjoying *Bliss.*

It confirmed for Morgan the absolute rightness of her making the break, learning to rely only on herself to feel good. Not her boyfriend. And not her mother, either.

Two and a half months into her teaching career and her new location in Canterbury, Morgan loved making her own decisions, living in her own home, even buying the groceries she liked without living in the shadow of a nose wrinkling in disapproval—*Do you know how many grams of sugar this has in it?*

Just as *Bliss* had promised, every day of being an independent woman who answered to no one but herself felt like a new adventure.

But now, as the man at the forge turned to her, Morgan was stunned to find she had no idea at all what the word *adventure* meant.

Though something in the buccaneer blackness of his eyes promised he knew all about adventures so dark and mysterious they could make a woman quiver.

One who wasn't newly dedicated to independent living.

Morgan fervently reminded herself of her most recent joy—the absolute freedom of picking out the funky purple sofa that Karl, and possibly her mother, too, would have hated. Amelia Ainsworthy, author of *Bliss,* had dedicated a whole chapter of the book to furniture selection and Morgan felt she had done her proud.

But now that moment seemed far less magical as this man, Nate Hathoway, stood regarding her, his eyes made blacker by the flicker of the firelight, his brows drawn down in a fierce lack of welcome that echoed the sign on the door, his stance the stance of a warrior. Hard. Cynical. Unwavering.

One hand, sinewy with strength, held a pair of tongs, metal glowed orange-hot at the end of them.

Morgan felt her breath catch in her throat.

Cecilia's father, Nate Hathoway, with his classic features, strong cheekbones, flawless nose, chiseled jaw, sensuously full lips, was easily the most handsome man she had ever set eyes on.

"Can't you read?" he growled at her. "I'm not open to the public."

His voice was rough, impatient and impossibly sexy. It shivered across the back of Morgan's neck like a touch.

Ignoring her, he placed the hot iron on an anvil, took a hammer and plied his strength to it. She watched, dazed, at the ripple of disciplined muscle as he forced the iron to his will. His will won, with ease.

"Um, Mr. Hathoway, I can read, and I'm not the public. I'm Cecilia's teacher."

The silence was long. Finally, his sigh audible, he said, "Ah. Mrs. McGuire." He shot her a look that seemed uncomfortably hostile and returned his attention to the metal. He doused it in a bath. It sizzled and hissed as it hit, and he turned his eyes back to her, assessing.

Maybe it was just because they were so dark that they seemed wicked, eyes that would belong to a highwayman, or a pirate, or an outlaw, not to the father of a fragile six-year-old girl.

Morgan drew in a deep breath. It was imperative that she remember the errand that had brought her here. The permission slip for Cecilia to participate in *The Christmas Angel* was in her coat pocket.

"It's Miss, actually. The kids insist on Mrs. I corrected them for the first few days, but I'm afraid I've given up. Everybody over the age of twenty-one is Mrs. to a six-year-old. Particularly if she's a teacher."

She felt as if she was babbling. She realized,

embarrassed, that it sounded as if she *needed* him to know she was single. Which she didn't, Amelia forgive her!

"*Miss* McGuire, then," he said, not a flicker in that stern face showing the slightest interest in her marital status.

He folded those muscular, extremely enticing arms over the massiveness of his chest, rocked back on his heels, regarded her coolly, *waiting,* the impatience not even thinly veiled.

"Morgan," she said. Why was she inviting him to call her by her first name? She told herself it was to see if she could get the barrier down in his eyes. Her mission here was already doomed if she could not get past that.

But part of her knew that wasn't the total truth. The total truth was that she did not want to be seen *only* as the new first-grade teacher, and all that implied, such as boring and prim. Part of her, weak as that part was, was clamoring for this man to see her as a woman.

There was an Amelia Ainsworthy in her head

frowning at her with at least as much disapproval as Karl ever had!

But that's what the devil did. Tempted. And looking at his lips, stern, unyielding, but somehow as sensual as his voice, she felt the most horrible shiver of temptation.

"It's obvious to me Cecilia is a child who is loved," Morgan said. It sounded rehearsed. It *was* rehearsed, and thank goodness she'd had the foresight to rehearse something, or despite her disciplined nightly reading of *Bliss,* Morgan would be standing here struck dumb by his gorgeousness and the fact he *exuded* male power.

Now, she wished she had rehearsed something without the word *love* in it.

Because isn't that what fallen angels like the man in front of her did? Tempted naive women to believe maybe love could soften something in that hard face, that maybe love could heal something that had broken?

He said nothing, but if she had hoped to soften him by telling him she knew he loved his daughter, it had not succeeded. The lines around his mouth deepened in an expression of impenetrable cynicism.

"Cecilia has the confidence and quickness of a child sure of her place in the world." Originally, Morgan had planned on saying something about that quickness being channeled somewhere other than Cecilia's fists, but now she decided to save that for a later meeting.

Which assumed there would be a later meeting, not that anything in his face encouraged such an assumption.

She had also planned on saying something like in light of the fact her mother had died, Cecilia's confidence and brightness spoke volumes of the parent left behind. But somehow, her instinct warned her not to speak of the death of his wife.

Though nothing in his body language, in the shuttered eyes, invited her to continue, Morgan pressed on, shocked that what she said next had nothing to do with the permission slip for *The Christmas Angel*.

"It's the *mechanics* of raising a child, and

probably particularly a girl child, that might be the problem for you, Mr. Hathoway."

It's none of your business, Mary Beth had warned her dourly when Morgan had admitted she might broach the subject while she was there about the permission slip. *You're here to teach, not set up family counseling services.*

Morgan did not think sending the odd note home qualified as family counseling services. Though Nate Hathoway's failure to respond to the notes should have acted as warning to back off, rather than invitation to step in.

Obviously, he was a man who did not take kindly to having his failings pointed out to him, because his voice was colder than the Connecticut wind that picked that moment to shriek under the eaves of the barn.

"Maybe you'd better be specific about the *problem,* Miss McGuire."

Cecilia needed her, and that made Morgan brave when it felt as if courage would fail her. "There have been some incidents of the other children making fun of Cecilia."

In half a dozen long strides he was across the floor of his workshop, and staring down at her with those mesmerizing, devil-dark eyes.

She could smell him, and the smell was as potent as a potion: the tangy smell of heat and hard work, molten iron, soft leather. *Man.*

"What kids?" he asked dangerously.

Morgan had to tilt her chin to look at him. She did not like it that his eyes had narrowed to menacing slits, that the muscle was jerking in the line of his jaw, or that his fist was unconsciously clenching and unclenching at his side.

This close to Nate Hathoway, she could see the beginning of dark whiskers shadowing the hollows of impossibly high cheekbones, hugging the cleft of his chin. It made him look even more roguish and untamable than he had looked from across the room.

His lips were so full and finely shaped that just looking at them could steal a woman's voice, her tongue could freeze to the roof of her mouth.

"It's not about the kids," she managed to stammer, ordering her eyes to move away from the pure sensual art of his mouth.

"The hell it isn't."

"You can't seriously expect me to name names."

"You tell me who is making fun of Ace, and I'll look after it. Since you haven't."

Morgan shivered at his accusing tone, but felt her own strength shimmer back to life, her backbone straightening. She was as protective as a mother bear with cubs. All of those children were her cubs. Sometimes, looking out at the tiny sea of eager faces in the morning, it still stunned her how tiny and vulnerable six-year-olds could be.

And, after a day like today, it stunned her how quickly all that innocence could turn to terror on wheels. Still, she was not going to sic him on *her* kids!

She took a deep breath, tried not to let her inner quiver at the expression on his face show. "We are talking about six-year-olds. How would you propose to look after that, Mr. Hathoway?"

"I wasn't going to hunt them down," he said, reading her trepidation, disdain that she would conclude such a thing in the husky, controlled tone of his voice. Still, he flexed one of the naked muscles of his biceps with leashed anger.

Morgan's eyes caught there. A bead of sweat was slipping down the ridge of a perfectly cut muscle. She had that tongue-frozen-against-the-roof-of-her-mouth feeling again. Thank goodness. Otherwise she might have involuntarily licked her lips at how damnably *tantalizing* every single thing about him was.

"I wouldn't deal with the children," he continued softly, "but I grew up with their parents. I could go have a little talking-to with certain people."

The threat was unmistakable. But so was the love and pure need to protect his daughter. It felt as if that love Nate Hathoway had for his daughter could melt Morgan as surely as that fire blazing in the background melted iron.

"Mr. Hathoway, you just need to take a few small steps at home to help her."

"Since you are unable to help her at school?"

The sensation of melting disappeared! So did the tongue-stuck-to-the-roof-of-her-mouth feeling. She was not going to be attacked!

"That's unfair!" She was pleased with how calm she sounded, so she continued. "I have twenty-two children in my class. I can't be with every single one of them every single second, monitoring what they are saying among themselves, or to Cecilia."

"What are they saying?"

There were old incidents she could bring up: the fun they had made of Cecilia's hair before he had cut it, how someone had cruelly noticed how attached she was to a certain dress. Though it was always clean it was faded from her wearing it again and again. With boys' hiking boots, instead of shoes. They were situations that had caused teasing. Cecilia was no doormat. She came out fighting, and looking at the man before her, Morgan was pretty sure where she'd learned that!

Still, Morgan had prided herself on creatively

finding a remedy for each situation. Only it was becoming disheartening how quickly it was replaced with a new situation.

Morgan had to get to the heart of the problem.

"Just for an example, this morning Cecilia arrived with a very, er, odd, hairstyle. I'm afraid it left her open to some teasing even before she revealed her secret holding ingredient."

"She told me it was hair gel."

"It was gel, but not hair gel."

He looked askance at her.

"She didn't know gel wasn't gel. She used gel toothpaste."

He said a word people generally avoided using in front of the first-grade teacher. And then he ran a hand through the thick darkness of his own hair. Her eyes followed that motion helplessly.

"Didn't you say anything to her about her hair before she left for school?" she managed to choke out.

"Yeah," he said ruefully, the faintest chink appearing in that armor. "I told her it looked sharp."

It had looked *sharp*. Literally. But if she planned to be taken seriously, Morgan knew now was not the time to smile.

"Mr. Hathoway, you cannot send your daughter to school with a shark fin on top of her head and expect she will not be teased!"

"How do I know what's fashionable in the six-year-old set?" he asked, and a second chink appeared in the armor. A truly bewildered look slipped by the remoteness in his dark eyes. "To be honest, her hair this morning seemed like an improvement on the raised-by-wolves look she was sporting before she finally let me talk her into cutting her hair."

Remembered hair battles flashed through his eyes, and Morgan found her gaze on those hands. It was too easy to imagine him trying to gentle his strength to deal with his daughter's unruly hair.

But the last thing Morgan needed to do was couple a feeling of tenderness with the animal pull of his male magnetism!

"It was not an improvement," she said firmly,

snippily, trying desperately to stay on track. "The children were merciless, even after I made it clear I wanted no comments made. The recess monitor told me Cecilia got called Captain Colgate, Toothpaste Princess and Miss Froggy Fluoride."

"I'll bet the froggy one was Bradley Campbell's boy," he said darkly. "Ace told me he's called her Miss Froggy before, because of her voice."

"Her voice is adorable. She'll outgrow that little croakiness," Morgan said firmly. "I've already spoken to Freddy about teasing her about it."

Nate glowered, unconvinced.

Morgan pressed on. "To make matters worse, today at lunch break someone noticed her overalls. They said she had stolen them, that they belonged to an older sister and they were missing."

"Somebody accused Ace of *stealing?*"

Morgan thought he was going to have problems with the joint in his jaw if he didn't find a different way to deal with tension.

"Cecilia said she had taken the overalls from the lost-and-found box."

"But why?" he asked, genuinely baffled.

"When's the last time you bought her clothes?" Morgan was aware of something gentling in her voice. "Mr. Hathoway, I sent you a note suggesting a shopping trip might be in order."

"I don't read your notes."

"Why not?"

"Because I don't need a little fresh-out-of-college snip like you telling me how to raise my daughter. Oh, and I also don't do shopping."

"Obviously! And your daughter has suffered as a consequence!"

He glared at her. A lesser woman might have just touched her forelock and bowed out the door.

But blessed—or cursed—with the newfound strength of a woman who was working her way through *Bliss* and making careful notations in the margins, and who had purchased a sofa in a rather adventurous shade of purple, she plunged on.

"Cecilia told me that's why she took the overalls from the lost-and-found box…to spare you a shopping trip. She doesn't have anything that fits properly. She wears the same favorites over and over. She wears hiking boots with skirts, Mr. Hathoway! Haven't you noticed that?"

He said that word again, and something besides hardness flickered in those eyes again. It was worse than the hardness. Pain so deep it was like a bottomless pool.

"I guess I didn't notice," he said, the warrior stance shifting ever so slightly, something defeated in his voice. "Ace could have said something."

"She seems to think if she asks nothing of you, she's protecting you in some way."

The smallest hint of a smile tickled across lips that had the potential to be so sexy they could make a woman's heart stop.

"She *is* protecting me in some way. Grocery shopping is tough enough. I have to go out of town for groceries to avoid recipe exchanges with well-meaning neighbors."

Whom, Morgan was willing to guess, were mostly female. And available. She could easily imagine him being swarmed at a market in a small town where everyone would know his history. Wife killed, nearly two years ago, Christmas Eve car accident. *Widower. Single dad.*

"The girl's department is impossible," he went on grimly. "A sea of pink. Women everywhere. Frills." He said that word again, softly, with pained remembrance shadowing his eyes. He shook his head. "I don't do shopping," he said again, firmly, resolutely.

"I'd be happy to take her shopping."

It was the type of offer that would have Mary Beth rolling her eyes. It was the type of offer that probably made Morgan's insanity certifiable. Could she tangle her life with those of the Hathoways without dancing with something very powerful and possibly not tamable?

But whatever brief humanity had touched Nate's features it was doused as carelessly as he had plunged that red-hot metal into water.

"I don't do pity, either."

Good, Morgan congratulated herself. She had done her best. She should leave now, while her dignity was somewhat in tact. Mary Beth would approve if she left without saying another single word.

Naturally, she didn't.

"It's not pity. I happen to love shopping. I can't think of anything I would consider more fun than taking Cecilia on a shopping excursion."

CHAPTER TWO

I CAN'T THINK of anything I would consider more fun than taking Cecilia on a shopping excursion.

Mary Beth is going to think I'm crazy, Morgan thought.

Plus, standing here in such close proximity to his lips, she could think of *one* thing that would be quite a bit more fun than taking Cecilia on a shopping excursion. Or maybe *two*.

"I'll look after it," Nate Hathoway said, coolly adding with formal politeness, "thanks for dropping in, Miss McGuire."

And then he dismissed her, strode back across his workshop and turned his back to her, faced the fire. He was instantly engrossed in whatever he was doing.

Morgan stared at him, but instead of leaving,

she marched over to one of the bins just inside the front door. It contained coat hooks, in black wrought iron.

She picked up a pair, loved the substance of them in her hands. In a world where everything was transient, everything was meant to be enjoyed for a short while and then replaced—like her purple sofa—the coat hooks felt as if they were made to last forever.

Not a word a newly independent woman wanted to be thinking of anywhere in the vicinity of Nate Hathoway.

Still, his work with the black iron was incredible, flawless. The metal was so smooth it might have been silk. The curve of the hanger seemed impossibly delicate. How had he wrought this from something as inflexible as iron?

"I'll trade you," Morgan said on an impulse.

He turned and looked at her.

"My time with your daughter for some of your workmanship." She held up the pair of coat hooks.

She could already picture them hanging inside

her front door, she already felt as if she *had* to have them. Even if he didn't agree to the trade, she would have to try and buy them from him.

But she saw she had found precisely the right way to get to him: a trade in no way injured his pride, which looked substantial. Plus, it got him out of the dreaded shopping trip to the girls' department.

He nodded, once, curtly. "Okay. Done."

She went to put the coat hooks back, until they worked out the details of their arrangement, but he growled at her.

"Take them."

"Saturday morning? I can pick Cecilia up around ten."

"Fine." He turned away from her again. She saw he was heating a rod of iron, and she wished she had the nerve to go watch how he worked his magic on it. But she didn't.

She turned and let herself quietly out the door. Only as she walked away did she consider that by taking the coat hangers, she had taken a piece of him with her.

Morgan was aware she would never be able to look at her new acquisition without picturing him, hammer in hand, and feeling the potent pull of the incredible energy he had poured, molten, into manufacturing the coat hangers.

"I wonder what I've gotten myself into?" she asked out loud, walking away from the old barn, the last of the leaves floated from the trees around her. And then she realized just how much Nate Hathoway had managed to rattle her when she touched a piece of paper in her coat pocket.

And realized it was the permission slip for *The Christmas Angel*, still unsigned.

"Ah, Ace," Nate said uneasily, "you know how I promised I'd take you to the antique-car show this morning?"

His daughter was busy coloring at the kitchen table, enjoying a Saturday morning in her jammies. They were faded cotton-candy pink. They had feet in them, which made her seem like a baby. His baby.

He felt a fresh wave of anger at the kids teasing

her. And fresh frustration at the snippy young teacher for thinking she knew everything.

He had tried to think about that visit from the teacher as little as possible, and not just because it made him acutely aware of his failings as a single parent.

No, the teacher had been pretty. Annoying, but pretty.

And when he thought of her, it seemed to be the *pretty* part he thought of—the lush auburn hair, the sparkling green eyes, the wholesome features, the delicate curves—rather than the annoying part.

Ace glanced up at him. Her shortened red hair was sticking up every which way this morning, still an improvement over the toothpaste fin of last week, and the long tangled mop he had tried to tame—unsuccessfully—before that.

"We're not going to the car show?" she asked.

Nate hated disappointing her. He had been mulling over how to break this to her. Which is probably why he hadn't told her earlier that her plans for Saturday were changed. Sometimes with Ace, it was better not to let her think things over for too long.

"We're not going to the car show?" she asked again, something faintly strident in her voice.

Just as he had thought. She was clearly devastated.

"Uh, no. Your teacher is coming over." He had an envelope full of cash ready to hand Morgan McGuire for any purchases she made for Ace. His guilt over changing the car-show plans was being balanced, somewhat, by the incredibly wonderful fact he didn't have to go shopping.

The devastation dissolved from her face. "Mrs. McGuire?" Ace whispered with reverence. "She's coming here?"

"It's not like it's a visit from the pope," he said, vaguely irritated, realizing he may have overestimated the attractions of the car show by just a little.

"What's a pope?"

"Okay, the queen, then."

"The queen's coming here?" Ace said, clearly baffled.

"No. Miss McGuire's coming here. She's going to take you shopping. Instead of me taking you to the car show."

The crayon fell out of Ace's fingers. "I'm going shopping with Mrs. McGuire? *Me?*" Her brown eyes got huge. She gave a little squeal of delight, got up and did a little dance around the kitchen, hugging herself. He doubted a million-dollar lottery winner could have outdone her show of exuberance.

Okay, he admitted wryly, so he had overestimated the appeal of the car show by quite a bit.

Nate felt a little smile tickle his own lips at his daughter's delight, and then chastised himself for the fact there had not been nearly enough moments like this since his wife had died. Slippery roads. A single vehicle accident on Christmas Eve, Cindy had succumbed to her horrific injuries on Christmas day. There was no one to blame.

No one to direct the helpless rage at.

Ace stopped dancing abruptly. Her face clouded and her shoulders caved in. It was like watching the air go out of a balloon, buoyancy dissolving into soggy, limp latex.

"No," Ace said, her voice brave, her chin quivering. "I'm not going to go shopping with Mrs. McGuire. I can't."

"Huh? Why?"

"Because Saturday is *our* day. Yours and mine, Daddy. Always. And forever."

"Well, just this once it would be okay—"

"No," she said firmly. "I'm not leaving you alone."

"I'll be okay, Ace. I can go to the car show by myself."

"Nope," she said, and then furiously insisted, "it's *our* day." She tried to smile, but wavered, and after struggling valiantly for a few seconds to hide the true cost of her sacrifice, she burst into tears and ran and locked herself in the bathroom.

"Come on, Ace," he said, knocking softly on

the bathroom door. "We can have *our* day tomorrow. I'll take you over to Aunt Molly's and you can ride Happy."

Happy was a chunky Shetland pony, born and bred in hell. Her Aunt Molly had given the pony to Ace for Christmas last year, a stroke of genius that had provided some distraction from the bitter memories of the day. Ace loved the evil dwarf equine completely.

But Happy was not providing the necessary distraction today. There was no answer from the other side of the bathroom door. Except sobbing. Nate realized it was truly serious when even the pony promise didn't work.

Nate knew what he had to do, though it probably spoke volumes to his character just how reluctant he was to do it.

"Maybe," he said slowly, hoping some miracle—furnace exploding, earthquake—could save him from finishing this sentence, "since it's our day, I could tag along on your shopping trip with Miss McGuire."

No explosion. No earthquake. The desperate

suggestion of a cornered man was uttered without intervention from a universe he already suspected was not exactly on his side.

Silence. And then the door opened a crack. Ace regarded him with those big moist brown eyes. Tears were beaded on her lashes, and her cheeks were wet.

"Would you, Daddy?" she whispered.

The truth was he would rather be staked out on an anthill covered in maple syrup than go shopping with Ace and her startlingly delectable teacher.

But he sucked it up and did what had to be done, wishing the little snip who was so quick to send the notes criticizing his parenting could see him manning up now.

"Sure," he said, his voice deliberately casual. "I'll go, too." Feeling like a man who had escaped certain torture, only to be recaptured, Nate slipped the envelope of shopping cash he had prepared for the teacher into his own pocket.

"Are you sure, Daddy?" Ace looked faintly skeptical. She knew how he hated shopping.

Enough to steal overalls to try and save him, he reminded himself. "I don't want to miss *our* day, either," he assured her.

Inwardly, he was plotting. This could be quick. A trip down to Canterbury's one-and-only department store, Finnegan's Mercantile, a beeline to girls' wear, a few sweat suits—Miss McGuire approved, probably in various shades of pink—stuffed into a carry basket and back out the door.

He hoped the store would be relatively empty. He didn't want rumors starting about him and the teacher.

It occurred to Nate, with any luck, they were still going to make the car show. His happiness must have shown on his face, because Ace shot out of the bathroom and wrapped sturdy arms around his waist.

"Daddy," she said, in that little frog croak of hers, staring up at him with adoration he was so aware of not deserving, "I love you."

Ace saved him from the awkwardness of his having to break it to Miss Morgan McGuire that he was accompanying them on their trip, by answering the doorbell on its first ring.

Freshly dressed in what she had announced was her *best* outfit—worn pink denims and a shirt that Hannah Montana had long since faded off—Ace threw open the front door.

"Mrs. McGuire," she crowed, "my daddy's coming, too! He's coming shopping with me and you."

And then Ace hugged herself and hopped around on one foot, while Morgan McGuire slipped in the door.

Nate was suddenly aware his housekeeping was not that good, and *annoyed* by his awareness of it. He resisted the temptation to shove a pair of his work socks, abandoned on the floor, under the couch with his foot.

It must be the fact she was a teacher that made him feel as if everything was being graded: newspapers out on the coffee table; a thin layer of dust on everything, unfolded laundry leaning out of a hamper balanced perilously on the arm of the couch.

At Ace's favorite play station, the raised fireplace hearth, there was an entire orphanage of naked dolls, Play-Doh formations long since cracked and hardened, a forlorn-looking green plush dog that had once had stuffing.

So instead of looking like he cared how Morgan McGuire felt about his house and his housekeeping—or lack thereof—Nate did his best to look casual, braced his shoulder against the door frame of the living room, and shoved his hands into the front of his jeans pockets.

Morgan actually seemed stunned enough by Ace's announcement that he would be joining them that she didn't appear to notice one thing about the controlled chaos of his housekeeping methods.

She was blushing.

He found himself surprised and reluctantly charmed that anyone blushed anymore, at least over something as benign as a shopping trip with a six-year-old and her fashion handicapped father.

The first-grade teacher was as pretty as he

remembered her, maybe prettier, especially with that high color in her cheeks.

"I'm surprised you'll be joining us," Morgan said to him, tilting her chin in defiance of the blush, "I thought you made your feelings about shopping eminently clear."

He shrugged, enjoying her discomfort over his addition to the party enough that it almost made up for his aversion to shopping.

Almost.

"I thought we'd go to the mall in Greenville," Morgan said, jingling her car keys in her hand and glancing away from him.

Why did it please him that he made her nervous? And how could he be pleased and annoyed at the same time? A trip to Greenville was a full-day excursion!

"I thought we were going to Finnegan's," he said. Why couldn't Ace have just been bribed with Happy time, same as always?

Why did he have an ugly feeling Morgan McGuire was the type of woman who changed *same as always?*

"Finnegan's?" Morgan said. "Oh." In the same tone one might use if a fishmonger was trying to talk them into buying a particularly smelly piece of fish. "There's not much in the way of selection there."

"But Greenville is over an hour and a half away!" he protested. By the time they got there, they'd have to have lunch. Even before they started shopping. He could see the car show slip a little further from his grasp.

And lunch with the first-grade teacher? His life, deliberately *same as always* since Cindy's death, was being hijacked, and getting more complicated by the minute.

"It's the closest mall," Morgan said, and he could see she had a stubborn bent to her that might match his own, if tested.

As if the careful script on the handwritten notes sent home hadn't been fair enough warning of that.

"And the best shopping."

"The best shopping," Ace breathed. "Could

we go to The Snow Cave? That's where Brenda Weston got her winter coat. It has white fur."

Nate shot his daughter an astonished look. This was the first time she'd ever indicated she knew the name of a store in Greenville, or that she coveted a coat that had white fur.

"Surrender to the day," he muttered sternly to himself, not that the word *surrender* had appeared in a Hathoway's vocabulary for at least two hundred years.

"Pardon?" Morgan asked.

"I said lead the way."

But when she did, he wasn't happy about that, either. She drove one of those teeny tiny cars that got three zillion miles per every gallon of gas.

There was no way he could sit in the sardine-can-size backseat, and if he got in the front seat, his shoulder was going to be touching hers.

All the way to Greenville.

And even if he was determined to surrender to the day, he was not about to *invite* additional assaults on his defenses.

"I've seen Tinkertoys bigger than this car," he muttered. "We'd better take my vehicle."

And there was something about Miss Morgan McGuire that already attacked his defenses. That made a part of him he thought was broken beyond repair wonder if there was even the slimmest chance it could be fixed.

Why would anyone in their right mind want to fix something that hurt so bad when it broke?

He realized he was thinking of his heart.

Stupid thoughts for a man about to spend an hour and a half in a vehicle—any vehicle—with someone as cute as Morgan McGuire. He was pretty sure it was going to be the longest hour and a half of his life.

Stupid thoughts for a man who had vowed when his wife died—and Hathoways took their vows seriously—that his heart was going to be made of the same iron he made his livelihood shaping.

Out of nowhere, a memory blasted him.

I wish you could know what it is to fall in love, Nate.

Stop it, Cin, I love you.

No. Head over heels, I can't breathe, think, function. That kind of fall-in-love.

Cindy had been his best friend's girl. David had joined the services and been killed overseas. For a while, it had looked like the grief would take her, too. But Nate had done what best friends do, what he had promised David. He had stepped in to look after her.

Can't breathe? Think? Function? That doesn't even sound fun to me.

She'd laughed. But sadly. *Hath, you don't know squat.*

There was a problem with vowing your heart was going to be made of iron, and Nate was aware of it as he settled in the driver's seat beside Morgan, and her delicate perfume surrounded him.

Iron had a secret. It was only strong until it was tested by fire. Heated hot enough it was as pliable as butter.

And someone like Morgan McGuire probably

had a whole lot more fire than her prim exterior was letting on.

But as long as he didn't have to touch her shoulder all the way to Greenville he didn't have to find out. He could make himself immune to her, despite the delicacy of her scent.

It should be easy. After all, Nate had made himself immune to every other woman who had come calling, thinking he and Ace needed sympathy and help, loving and saving.

He didn't need anything. From anyone. And in that, he took pride.

And some days it felt like pride—and Ace— were all he had left.

But even once they were all loaded into his spacious SUV, even though his shoulder was not touching Morgan's, Nate was totally aware of her in the passenger seat, turning around to talk to Ace.

And he was aware the trip to Greenville had never gone by more quickly.

Because Morgan had switched cars, but not intent. And Nate saw she was intent on making the day fun for Ace, and her genuine caring for his daughter softened him toward her in a way he did not want to be softened.

For as much as he resisted her attempts to involve him, it made Nate mildly ashamed that on a long car trip with Ace he had a tendency to plug a movie into the portable DVD player.

Nate glanced over at Morgan. Her eyes had a shine to them, a clearness, a trueness.

He was aware that since the death of Cindy he had lived in the darkness of sorrow, in the grip of how helpless he had been to change anything at a moment when it had really counted.

Morgan's light was not going to pierce that. He wasn't going to allow it.

"With an oink, oink here, and an oink, oink there," Morgan McGuire sang with enthusiasm that made up for a surprisingly horrible voice.

It was written all over her that she was young and innocent and completely naive. That she had never known hardship like his own hardscrabble upbringing at a forge that was going broke, that she had been untouched by true tragedy.

"Oink," she invited him, and then teased, "you look like you would make a terrific pig."

He hoped that wasn't a dig at his housekeeping, but again he was taken by the transparency in her face. Morgan McGuire appeared to be the woman least likely to make digs.

"—here an oink, there an oink, everywhere an oink, oink—"

He shook his head, refusing to be drawn into her world. No good could come from it. When soft met hard, soft lost.

The best thing he could ever do for this teacher who cared about his daughter with a genuineness he could not deny, was to make sure he didn't repay her caring by hurting her.

And following the thin thread of attraction he could feel leaping in him as her voice and her scent and her enthusiasm for oinking filled his vehicle, could only end in that one place.

And he was cynical enough to know that.

Even if she wasn't.

* * *

Morgan glanced across the restaurant table at Nate Hathoway. Nothing in the time they had spent in the truck lessened her first impression of him standing alone bending iron to his will.

He was a warrior. Battle-scarred, self-reliant, his emotions contained behind walls so high it would be nearly impossible to scale them.

So, being Morgan, naturally she tried to scale them anyway.

She had been aware that she was trying to make him smile as they had traveled, deliberately using her worst singing voice, trying to get him to participate. She told herself it was so Ace could see a softer side of her father, but she knew that wasn't the entire truth.

She had seen a tickle of a smile at his forge on their first meeting. She wanted to see if she could tempt it out again.

But she had failed. The more she tried, the more he had tightened his cloak of remoteness around himself.

Though Morgan had not missed how his eyes found Ace in the rearview mirror, had not missed he was indulging her antics because his daughter was enjoying them.

Really, Nate Hathoway was the man least likely to ever be seen at a Cheesie Charlie's franchise, but here he was, tolerating a noise level that was nothing less than astonishing, his eyes unreadable when the menus were delivered by a guy in a somewhat the worse-for-wear chicken suit.

He ate the atrocious food without comment, slipped the waiter-chicken a tip when he came to their table and serenaded them with a song with Ace's name liberally sprinkled throughout.

"Well, wasn't that fun?" Morgan asked as they left Cheesie Charlie's.

"Yes!" Ace crowed. Even she seemed to notice that nothing was penetrating the hard armor around her father. "Daddy," she demanded, "didn't you think that was fun?"

"Fun as pounding nails with my forehead," he muttered.

"That doesn't sound fun," Ace pointed out.

"You're right," he said, and then sternly warned, "don't try it at home."

Morgan sighed as Ace skipped ahead to where they had parked. "How did you allow yourself to get talked into coming? I'm beginning to see you did not volunteer for this excursion."

He hesitated, and then he nodded at Cecilia. "We always spend Saturday together. It's our tradition. Since her mom passed. I was willing to forgo it, just this once. She wasn't."

"Somewhere under that hard exterior is there a heart of pure gold, Nate Hathoway?"

She finally got the smile, only it wasn't the one she'd been trying for. Cynical. Something tight around the edges of it. His eyes shielded.

"Don't kid yourself."

Instead of scaling his wall, she'd managed to get him to put it up higher! And for some reason it made her mad. If she couldn't make him laugh, then she might as well torment him.

"If you thought Cheesie Charlie's was fun, you're going to love The Snow Cave," Morgan promised him.

He gave her a dark, lingering look that sent shivers from her ears to her toes.

The Snow Cave proudly proclaimed itself as haute tot.

If he had looked out of place at Cheesie's, Nate Hathoway now looked acutely out of place in the exclusive girls' store. He was big and rugged amongst the racks and displays of pint-size *frilly* clothing in more shades of pink than Morgan was certain the male mind could imagine.

Ignoring his discomfort, at the same time as enjoying it immensely, Morgan sorted through the racks until she had both her and Cecilia's arms heaped up with selections: blouses and T-shirts, socks, slacks, dresses, skirts.

"Great," he said when it was obvious they could not carry one more thing. "Are you done? Can we go?"

"She has to try everything on."

"What?" He looked like a wolf caught in a trap. "What for? Just buy it all so we can leave."

Not even a little ashamed for enjoying his misery so thoroughly, Morgan leaned close to him and whispered, "This store is very expensive.

You should allow her to pick one or two items from here and we'll get the rest elsewhere."

"Elsewhere?" He closed his eyes and bit back a groan. "Just buy the damn stuff. I don't care what it costs. I don't want to go *elsewhere*."

She waited to feel guilty, but given how easily he had resisted her efforts to charm, she didn't.

Not in the least. This was a show of spunky liberation from needing his approval that even Amelia would have approved of!

"That's not how it works," Morgan said firmly. "We've been shopping for all of ten minutes. Don't be such a baby."

His mouth dropped open in shock, closed again. Morgan was sure she could hear him grinding his teeth before he finally said, "A *baby?* Me?"

"And could you try not to curse? Cecilia tends to bring some of your words to school."

"You consider *damn* a curse?" he said, clearly as astonished by that as by the fact that she'd had the audacity to call him a baby.

"I do," she said bravely.

He stared at her as if she was freshly minted

from a far-off planet. He scowled. He shoved his hands in the pockets of his jeans. He looked longingly at the door. And then Ace danced up, with one more *find*.

"Look! Sparkle skinny jeans that will fit me!"

He sighed with long suffering, shot Morgan a dark look that she answered with a bland, uncaring smile, and then allowed Ace to take his hand and tug him toward the change area.

Which, like everything at The Snow Cave, was designed to delight little girls. The waiting area, newly decorated for Christmas, was like the throne room in a winter palace fantasy.

And so there sat Nate Hathoway front row and center, in a pink satin chair which looked as if it could snap into kindling under his weight. But as Cecilia danced out in each of her new outfits, the scowl dissolved from his face, and even if he didn't smile, his expression was at least less menacing.

It was hours later that they finally drove through the darkness toward Canterbury and home. Ace fell asleep in her booster seat in the back instantly, nearly lost amongst the clothing bags and shoe boxes that surrounded her. They could have gone in the back of Nate's huge SUV, but she had insisted she had to have each of her purchases close to her.

Ace wore her new coat: an impractical pure-white curly fur creation that was going to make her the absolute envy of the grade-one girls. She had on a hair band with a somewhat wilted bow, and little red patent-leather shoes on her leotarded feet.

"She's worn right out," Nate said with a glance in the rearview mirror. "And no wonder. Is the female of the species born with an ability to power shop?"

"I think so."

"So how come you didn't get anything for yourself?"

"Because today wasn't about me."

He glanced at her, and she saw a warmth had crept past his guard and into his eyes. But he looked quickly away, before she could bask in it for too long.

Looking straight ahead, as snow was beginning to fall gently, Nate turned on the radio. It was apparently preset to a rock station, but he glanced at the sleeping girl, and then at Morgan, and fiddled with the dial until he found a soft country ballad.

"Why do you call Cecilia 'Ace'?" Morgan asked.

He hesitated, as if he did not want to reveal one single thing about himself or his family to her.

But then he said, "Her mom had started calling her Sissy, short for Cecilia, I guess. There are no sissies in the Hathoway family. Nobody was calling my kid Sissy."

And then he sighed. "I regret making an issue over it, now."

Morgan heard lots of regret in his voice. She had heard about the accident, and knew one minute he'd had a wife, and a life, and the next that everything had changed forever. What were his regrets? Had he called, *I love you,* as his wife had headed out the door for the last time?

His face was closed now, as if he already had said way more than he wanted to. Which meant he was the strong one who talked to no one about his pain.

She wanted to reach across the darkness of the cab, and invite him to tell her things he had told no one else, but she knew he would not appreciate the gesture.

Silence fell over them. Despite the quiet, there was something good about driving through the night with him, the soft music, the snow falling outside, his scent tickling at her nose.

Normally, particularly if she was driving by herself, the snow would have made Morgan nervous, but tonight she had a feeling of being with a man who would keep those he had been charged with guarding safe no matter what it took, no matter what it cost him.

But he hadn't, and he wore that failure to protect his wife around him like a cloak of pure pain.

Even though Morgan knew he had not been there at the accident that killed his wife, she was certain he would in some way hold himself responsible. Did he think he should have driven her that night? Not let her go into the storm?

She could not ask him that. Not yet. Which meant she thought someday maybe she could. Why was she hoping this shopping trip was not the end of it?

Because she felt so safe driving with him through the snow-filled night?

Amelia wouldn't have approved, but it was nice to rely on someone else's competence. Even though it might be weak, Morgan felt herself savoring the feeling of being looked after.

She glanced at his strong features, illuminated by the dash lights. He looked calm, despite the snowfall growing heavier outside, the windshield wipers slapping along trying to keep up.

Nate Hathoway might not smile much, but Morgan suddenly knew if your back was against the wall and barbarians were coming at you with knives in their teeth, he was the one you would want standing right beside you.

It was weariness that had allowed an independent woman such as herself to entertain such a traitorous thought, Morgan defended herself. And then, as if to prove it, the warmth inside the vehicle, the radio, the mesmerizing fall of snow—and the sense of being safe and taken care of—made it impossible for her to think of clever things to say. Or even to keep her eyes open.

When she woke up, it was to absolute stillness. The sound of the radio was gone, the vehicle had stopped moving, the dashboard lights were off, and the vehicle was empty.

She realized there was a weight on her shoulder, and that it was his hand, not shaking her, just touching her.

Even through the puffiness of her parka, she could feel his warmth, and his strength. It made her want to go back to sleep.

"Morgan, we're home."

For home to be a place shared, instead of a

place of aloneness, felt like the most alluring dream of all.

Recognizing her groggy vulnerability, Morgan shook herself awake. He was standing at her side of the SUV, the door open.

A quick glance showed the back was empty of every parcel and package. Ace was gone.

"Put her in bed," he said before Morgan asked. "Thought you might wake up as I moved stuff and the vehicle cooled off, but you were sleeping hard."

Morgan felt herself blushing. She'd obviously slept like a rock. She hoped she hadn't drooled and muttered his name in her sleep. Had she dreamed of the smile she had tried so hard—and failed—to produce?

And then suddenly, when she least expected it, it was there.

He was actually smiling at her. A small smile, but so genuine it was like the sun coming out on a dreary day. He reached out and touched her cheek.

"You've got the print of the seat cover across your cheek."

And then his hand dropped away, and he looked away.

"Miss McGuire?"

"Morgan."

He looked right at her. The smile was gone. "You gave my daughter a gift today. I haven't seen her so happy for a long, long time. I thank you for that."

And then, he bent toward her, brushed the print on her cheek again, and kissed the place on her cheek where his fingers had been. His lips were gloriously soft, a tenderness in them that belied every single thing she thought she had ever seen in his eyes.

And then Nate turned away from her, went up the walk to his house and into it, shut the door without once looking back.

She sat in his truck stunned, wondering if she had dreamed that moment, but finally managed to stir herself, shut the door of his vehicle and get into her own.

The night was so bright and cold and star-filled. Was she shivering from the cold, or from the absence of the warmth she had felt when he had touched his lips to her cheek?

It wasn't until she was nearly home that she realized that while she slept he had done more than empty his vehicle of parcels, and carry a sleeping Ace to her bedroom. Morgan saw he had put two more of the coat hangers on her front seat.

And she remembered she still had not gotten the permission slip for *The Christmas Angel* signed.

And she knew it was weak, and possibly stupid, and she knew it went against every single thing she had decided for herself when she had moved to Canterbury. It challenged every vow she had made as she devoured chapter after chapter of *Bliss: The Extraordinary Joy of Being a Single Woman.*

But Morgan still knew that she would use that unsigned permission slip as an excuse to see him again.

CHAPTER THREE

HE NEVER WANTED TO see her again.

Morgan McGuire was stirring things up in Nate Hathoway that did not need stirring.

That impulse to kiss her cheek was the last impulse he intended to follow. It had been like kissing the petals of a rose, so soft, so yielding. Touching the exquisite softness of her with his lips had made him acutely aware of a vast empty spot in his life.

As had spending a day with her, her laughter, her enthusiasm, contagious.

So, it was an easy decision. No more Morgan McGuire.

Nate, alone in his workshop, vowed it out loud. "I won't see her again. Won't have anything to do with her."

There. His and Ace's lives felt complicated

enough without adding the potential messiness of a relationship with the teacher.

Relationship? That was exactly why he wasn't seeing her again. A day—shopping of all things—made him think of the sassy schoolteacher in terms of a relationship?

No. He was setting his mind against it, and that was that.

One thing every single person in this town knew about Nate Hathoway: his discipline was legendary. When he said something, it happened.

It was that kind of discipline that had allowed him to take a forge—a relic from a past age that had not provided a decent living for the past two generations of Hathoway blacksmiths—and bend it to his vision for its future.

His own father had been skeptical, but then he was a Hathoway, and skepticism ran deep through the men in this family. So did hard work and hell-raising.

Cindy and David had been raised in the same kind of families as his. Solidly blue-collar, poor, proud. The three of them had been the musketeers, their friendship shielding them from the scorn of their wealthier classmates.

While his solution to the grinding poverty of his childhood had been the forge, David's had been the army. He felt the military would be his ticket to an education, to being able to provide for Cindy after he married her.

Instead, he'd come home in a flag-draped box.

You look after her if anything happens to me.
And so Nate had.

She'd never been quite the same, some laughter gone from her forever, but the baby had helped. Still, they had had a good relationship, a strong partnership, loyalty to each other and commitment to family.

Her loss had plunged him into an abyss that he had been able to avoid when David had died. Now he walked with an ever present and terrifying awareness that all a man's strength could not protect those he loved entirely. A man's certainty in his ability to control his world was an illusion.

A man could no more hold back tragedy than he could hold back waves crashing onto a shore.

Nate felt Cindy's loss sharply. But at the same time he felt some loss of himself.

Still, thinking of her now, Nate was aware Cindy would never have flinched from such a mild curse as *damn*.

And he was almost guiltily aware Cindy's scent permeating the interior of a vehicle had never filled him with such an intense sense of longing. For things he couldn't have.

Someone like Morgan McGuire could never fit into his world. His was a world without delicacy, since Cindy's death it had become even more a man's world.

"So, no more."

What about Ace in this world that was so without soft edges?

Well, he told himself, it *had* changed from the world of his childhood. It wasn't hardscrabble anymore. It wasn't the grinding poverty he had grown up with. The merciless teasing from his childhood—about his worn shoes, faded shirts, near-empty lunchbox—sat with him still. And made him proud.

And mean if need be.

Not that there had been even a hint of anyone looking down their noses at him for a long, long time.

Partly in respect for his fists.

Mostly because within two years of Nate taking over the forge—pouring his blood and his grit and his pure will into it—it had turned around.

The success of the forge was beyond anything he could have imagined for himself. He did commissions. He had custom orders well into next year. He sold his stock items as fast as he could make them.

Nate's success had paid off the mortgages on this property, financed his parents' retirement to Florida, allowed him things that a few years ago he would have considered unattainable luxuries. He could have any one of those antique cars he liked when he decided which one he wanted. He even had a college fund for Ace.

Still, there was no room for a woman like Morgan McGuire in his world.

Because he had success. And stuff.

And those things could satisfy without threatening, without coming close to that place inside of him he did not want touched.

But she could touch it. Morgan McGuire could not only touch it, but fill it. Make him aware of empty spaces he had been just as happy not knowing about.

He was suddenly aware she was there, in the forge, as if thinking about her alone could conjure her.

How did he know it was her?

A scent on the air, a feeling on the back of his neck as the door had opened almost silently and then closed again?

No. She was the only one who had ever ignored that Go Away sign.

Now, based on the strength of their shared shopping trip—and probably on that kiss he so regretted—she came right up to the hearth, stood beside him, watching intently as he worked.

Her perfume filled his space, filled him with that same intense longing he had become aware of in the truck. What was it, exactly? A promise of softness? He steeled himself against it, squinted into the fire, used the bellows to raise the heat and the flames yet higher.

Only then did he steal a glance at her. Nate willed himself to tell her to go away, and was astonished that his legendary discipline failed him. Completely.

Morgan's luscious auburn hair was scooped back in a ponytail that was falling out. The light from the flame made the strands of red shine with a life of their own.

The schoolteacher had on no makeup, but even without it her eyes shimmered a shade of green so pure that it put emeralds to shame. She did have something on her lips that gave them the most enticing little shine. She watched what he was doing without interrupting, and somehow his space did not feel compromised at all by her being here.

"Hi," he heard himself saying. Not exactly friendly, but not *go away,* either.

"Hi. What are you making?"

"It's part of a wrought iron gate for the entrance of a historic estate in Savannah, Georgia. A commission."

"It's fantastic." She had moved over to parts he had laid out on his worktable, piecing it together like a puzzle before assembling it.

He glanced at her again, saw she must have walked here. She was bundled up against the cold in a pink jacket and mittens that one of her students could have worn. Her cheeks glowed from being outside.

Nate saw how deeply she meant it about his work. His work had been praised by both artists and smithies around the world.

It grated that her praise meant so much. No wonder she had all those first graders eating out of the palm of her hand.

"I just wanted to drop by and let you know what a good week it's been for Cecilia."

"Because of the clothes?" he asked, and then

snorted with disdain. "We live in a superficial world when six-year-olds are being judged by their fashion statements, Miss Morgan."

He was aware, since he hadn't just told her out and out to *go away,* of wanting to bicker with her, to get her out that door one way or another.

Because despite his legendary discipline, being around her made that yearning nip at him, like a small aggravating dog that wouldn't be quiet.

But she didn't look any more perturbed by his deliberate cynicism than she had when she told him not to cuss. "It's not just because of the clothes, but because she feels different. Like she fits in. It's given her confidence."

"I have confidence. I never had nice clothes growing up."

Now why had he gone and said that? He glanced at her. Her eyes were on him, soft, inviting him to say more.

Which he wasn't going to!

"Thanks for dropping by. And the Ace update. You could have sent a note."

She still looked unoffended. In fact, she smiled. He wished she wouldn't do that. Smile.

It made him want to lay every hurt he had ever felt at her feet.

"We both know you don't read my notes."

If he promised he would read them from now on would she go away? He doubted it.

"I actually needed to see you. I need you to sign this permission slip for Cecilia to participate in *The Christmas Angel*. Rehearsals will be starting next week."

"I'm sick of hearing about *The Christmas Angel*," he said gruffly. "The whole town has gone nuts. I don't like Christmas. I don't like Wesley Wellhaven. And I really don't like *The Christmas Angel*."

She was silent for a moment. A sane person would have backed out the door and away from his show of ire. She didn't.

"Perhaps you should post a Grinch Lives Here sign above your Go Away sign."

"My wife was in an accident on Christmas Eve. She died on Christmas Day. It will be two years this year. Somehow that takes the ho-ho-ho out of the season."

He said it flatly, but he knew, somehow, despite his resolve to be indifferent to Morgan, he wasn't.

He didn't want her sympathy. He hated sympathy.

It was something else he wanted from her. When he put his finger on it, it astonished him. To not be so alone with it anymore.

To be able to tell someone that he had not been able to stop Cindy's excruciating pain. That he had been relieved when she died because she didn't have to be in pain anymore.

That through all that pain, she had looked *pleased* somehow, going to be with the one she truly loved. And through all that pain, she had looked at him and said finally, seconds before she died, with absolute calm and absolute certainty, *You've been my angel, Hath. Now I'll be yours.*

And he hated that he wanted to tell Morgan McGuire that, as if it was any of her business.

He hated that he wanted to tell her if Cindy was his angel, he'd seen no evidence of it, as if she, the know-it-all teacher, should be able to explain that to him. Wanting to tell her felt like a terrible weakness in a world built on pure strength.

Morgan moved back over to him until she stood way too close, gazing up at him with solemn green eyes that looked as if she could explain the impossible to him.

"I'm so sorry about your wife."

If she added a *but* as in *but it's time to get over it,* or for *Ace's sake* he would have the excuse he needed to really, really dislike her. He waited, aware he was hoping.

She said nothing.

Instead, without taking her eyes from him, she laid her hand on his wrist, something in that touch so tender it felt as if it would melt him, as surely as his fire-tempered steel.

She seemed to realize she was touching him, and that it might not be appropriate at the same time he jerked his arm away from her.

Brusquely, Nate said, "We won't be here for

Christmas. So there's no sense Ace getting involved in the Christmas-production thing. I'm taking her to Disneyland."

He made it sound as if he had been planning it forever, not as if he had just pulled it from the air, right this very moment, a plot to thwart her.

She didn't seem fooled.

"You know," she said softly, after a time, "this town is really suffering as a result of the downturn in the economy. Last year's concert, *The Christmas Miracle*, in Mountain Ridge, Vermont? The production alone pumped a lot of money into the town. But they couldn't have bought that kind of publicity. The filming of some of the winter scenery around that gorgeous little town sent people there in droves at a time of year when they don't usually get tourists."

"And that has what to do with me? And Ace?"

"The same could happen for Canterbury."

"So what?" he asked.

"It seems to me," she said softly, and if she was intimidated by his show of ill temper, she was not backing away from it, "that people need something to hope for. At Christmas more than any other time. They need to believe everything is going to be all right."

"Do they now?" How could she be that earnest? How could she be so sure of what people needed? Why did he think, given a chance, she could show him what he needed, too?

The fire was fine. He picked up the bellows anyway, focused on it, made the bellows huff and the fire roar, but not enough to shut out her voice.

"Ace needs to believe," Morgan continued softly. "She needs to believe that everything is going to be all right. And somehow I don't think that belief will be nurtured by an escape to Disneyland, as pleasant a distraction as that may be."

He put down the bellows. This had gone far enough, really. He turned to her, head-on, folded his arms over his chest. "This is beginning to sound depressingly like one of your notes. How did you get to know what the whole world needs?

How do you get to be so smart for someone so wet behind the ears, fresh out of college?"

She blushed, but it was an angry blush.

Finally, he'd accomplished what he wanted. He was pushing her away. Straight out the door. Never to return, with any luck. Nate was aware that accomplishing his goal didn't feel nearly as satisfying as he thought it would.

"Somehow," she said, surprising him by matching his battle stance, folding her arms over her chest and facing him instead of backing away, "even though you have suffered tragedy, Nate, I would have never pegged you as the kind of man who would be indifferent to the woes of your neighbors. And their hopes."

His mouth opened.

And then closed.

How had a discussion about a damned permission slip turned into this? A soul search? A desire to be a better man.

And not just for his daughter.

Oh, no, it would be easy if it was just for his

daughter. No, it was for her, too. Miss Snippy Know-It-All.

"I'll think about it," he said.

The famous line was always used, by everyone including him, as a convenient form of dismissal. What it really meant was *No, and I don't ever intend to think about this again.*

This time he knew he wasn't going to be so lucky.

"It means a lot to Ace to be in that production," Morgan said. "I already told the kids in my class we were all doing it, or none of us were."

"Nothing like a little pressure," he replied, turning away from her now, picking up his tongs, taking the red-hot rod of iron from the fire. "Are you telling me the Christmas joy of a dozen and a half six-year-olds relies on me?"

He glanced at her, and she nodded solemnly, ignoring his deliberately skeptical tone.

"That's a scary thing," he told her quietly, his voice deliberately loaded with cynicism. "Nearly as scary as the hope of the whole town resting on my shoulders."

She didn't have the sense to flinch from his sarcasm. He was going to have to lay it out nice and plain for her. "I'm the wrong man to trust with such things, Miss McGuire."

She looked at him for a long time as he began to hammer out the rod, and then just as he glanced at her, eyebrows raised, looking askance as if *Oh, are you still here?* she nodded once, as if she knew something about him he did not know himself.

"I don't think you are the wrong man to trust," she said softly. "I think you just wish you were."

And having looked right into his soul, Little Miss Snip removed the permission slip from her pink coat pocket, set it on his worktable, smoothed it carefully with her hand, and then turned on her heel and left him there to brood over his fire.

A little while later, in the house, getting dinner ready—hot dogs and a salad—he said to Ace, in his I-just-had-this-great-idea voice, "Ace, what would you think of a trip to Disneyland over Christmas?"

The truth was, he expected at least the exuberant dance that the shopping trip with Morgan McGuire had elicited. Instead there was silence.

He turned from the pot on the stove after prodding a frozen hot dog with a fork, as if that would get it to cook quicker, and looked at his daughter.

Ace was getting her hot-dog bun ready, lots of ketchup and relish, not dancing around at all. Today she was wearing her new skirt, the red one with the white pom-poms on the hem. She looked adorable. He hoped that didn't mean boys would start coming by here. No, surely that worry was years away.

"Disneyland?" he said, wondering if she was daydreaming and hadn't heard him.

"Oh, Daddy," she said with a sigh of long suffering, in her *you're so silly* voice. "We can't go to Disneyland over Christmas. I *have* to be in *The Christmas Angel*. It's on Christmas Eve.

It's on TV, *live*. I should phone Grandma and Grandpa and tell them I'm going to be on TV."

Then in case he was getting any other bright ideas, she told him firmly, "And I don't want to go after, either. Brenda is having a skating party on Boxing Day. I hope I get new skates for Christmas. When am I going to see Santa?"

He was pretty sure Ace and Brenda had been mortal enemies a week ago. So, Morgan had been right. Superficial or not, the clothes helped. His daughter was having a good week.

That was worth something. So was the light in her eyes when she talked about being on television.

Nate made a promise as soon as Santa set up at Finnegan's they would go, and then he made a mental note about the skates. Then once she was in bed, he took the permission slip, signed it and shoved it into Ace's backpack.

It didn't feel like nearly the concession it should have. He told himself it had nothing to do with Morgan McGuire and everything to do with Ace.

An hour after Ace was in bed, his phone rang. It was Canterbury's mayor, who also owned the local gas station. *The Christmas Angel* needed skilled craftspeople to volunteer to work on the set. Would he consider doing it?

Before Morgan had arrived this afternoon his answer would have been curt and brief.

Now he was aware he did not want to be a man indifferent to the hopes and dreams of his neighbors.

What had she said? *I don't think you are the wrong man to trust, I think you just wish you were.*

It irked him that she was right. He should say no to this request just to spite her. But he didn't.

Small towns were strange places. Centuries-old feuds were put aside if tragedy struck.

Four generations of Hathoways had owned this forge and as far as Nate could tell they'd always been renegades and rebels. They didn't go to church, or belong to the PTA or the numerous Canterbury service clubs. Hardworking but hell-raising, they were always on the fringe of the community. His family, David's and Cindy's.

And yet, when David had died, the town had given him the hero's send-off that he deserved.

And their support had been even more pronounced after Cindy had died. Nate's neighbors had gathered around him in ways he would have never expected. A minister at a church he had never been to had offered to do the service; there had not been enough seats for everyone who came to his wife's funeral.

People who he would have thought did not know of his existence—like the man who had just phoned him—had been there for him and for Ace unconditionally, wanting nothing in return, not holding his bad temper or his need to deal with his grief alone against him.

Sometimes, still, he came to the house from the forge to find an anonymous casserole at the door, or fresh-baked cookies, or a brand-new toy or outfit for Ace.

At first it had been hard for him to accept, but at some time Nate had realized it wasn't charity. It was something deeper than that. It was why people chose to live in small communities. To know they were cared about, that whether you wanted it or not, your neighbors had your back.

And you didn't just keep taking that. In time, when you were ready, you offered it back.

Nate wasn't really sure if he was ready, but somehow it felt as if it was time to find out. And so that awareness of "something deeper" was how he found himself saying yes to the volunteer job of helping to build sets.

Since the school auditorium was the only venue big enough to host *The Christmas Angel,* Nate knew it was going to put him together again with Morgan McGuire. He knew it was inevitable that their lives were becoming intertwined. Whether he liked it or not.

And for a man who had pretty established opinions on what he liked and what he didn't, Nate Hathoway was a little distressed to find he simply didn't know if he liked it or not.

* * *

Morgan marched her twenty-two charges into the gymnasium. The truth was, after being so stern with Nate about the benefits of *The Christmas Angel* coming to Canterbury, she was beginning to feel a little sick of the whole thing herself.

The children talked of nothing else. They all thought their few minutes on television, singing backup to Wesley Wellhaven, meant they were going to be famous. They all tried to sing louder than the person next to them. Some of them were getting quite theatrical in their delivery of the songs.

The rehearsal time for the three original songs her class would sing was eating into valuable class time that Morgan felt would be better used for teaching fundamental skills, reading, writing and arithmetic.

Today was the first day her kids would be showing *The Christmas Angel* production team what they had learned. Much of the team had arrived last week, filling up the local hotel. Now *The Christmas Angel*'s own choir director, Mrs. Wesley Wellhaven herself, had arrived in town last night and would be taking over rehearsing the children.

As soon as Morgan entered the auditorium—which was also the school gymnasium, not that it could be used for that because of all the work going on getting the only stage in town ready for Wesley—Morgan *knew* he was here.

Something happened to her neck. It wasn't so sinister as the hackles rising, it was more as if someone sexy had breathed on her.

She looked around, and sure enough, there Nate was, helping another man lift a plywood cutout of a Christmas cottage up on stage.

At the same time as herding her small charges forward Morgan unabashedly took advantage of the fact Nate had no idea she was watching him, to study him, which was no mean feat given that Freddy Campbell kept poking Brenda Weston in the back, and Damien Dorchester was deliberately treading on Benjamin Chin's heels.

"Freddy, Damien, stop it." The correction was absent at best.

Because it seemed as if everything but *him* had

faded as Morgan looked to the stage. Nate had looked sexy at his forge, and he looked just as sexy here, with his tool belt slung low on the hips his jeans rode over, a plain T-shirt showing off the ripple of unconscious muscle as he lifted.

Let's face it, Morgan told herself, he'd look sexy no matter where he was, no matter what he was wearing, no matter what he was doing.

He was just a blastedly sexy man.

And yet there was more than sexiness to him.

No, there was a quiet and deep strength evident in Nate Hathoway. It had been there at Cheesie Charlie's, it had been there when he sat in the pink satin chair at The Snow Cave. And it was there now as he worked, a self-certainty that really was more sexy than his startling good looks.

Mrs. Wellhaven, a pinch-faced woman of an indeterminate age well above sixty, called the children up onto the stage, and the workers had to stop to let the kids file onto the triple-decker stand that had been built for them.

"Hi, Daddy!" Ace called.

"Yes," Mrs. Wellhaven said, lips pursed, "let's deal with that first off, shall we? Please do not call out the names of people you know as you come on the stage. Not during rehearsal, and God knows, not during the live production."

Ace scowled. Morgan glanced at Nate. Father's and child's expressions were identically mutinous.

Morgan shivered. In the final analysis could there be anything more sexy than a man who would protect his own, no matter what?

Still, the choir director had her job to do, and since Nate looked as if maybe he was going to go have a word with her, Morgan intercepted him.

"Hi. How are you?"

Though maybe it was just an excuse.

In all likelihood Nate was not going to berate the choir director.

"Who does she think she is telling my kid she can't say hi to me?" he muttered, mutiny still written all over his handsome face.

Or maybe he had been.

"You have to admit it might be a little chaotic if all the kids started calling greetings to their parents, grandparents and younger siblings on national live television," Morgan pointed out diplomatically.

He looked at her as if he had just noticed her. When Nate gave a woman his full attention, she didn't have a chance. That probably included the crotchety choir director.

"Ah, Miss McGuire, don't you ever get tired of being right all the time?" he asked her, folding his arms over the massiveness of his chest.

She had rather hoped they were past the *Miss McGuire* stage. "Morgan," she corrected him.

Mrs. Wellhaven cleared her throat, tipped her glasses and leveled a look at them. "Excuse me. We are trying to concentrate here." She turned back to the children. "I am Mrs. Wellhaven." Then she muttered, tapping her baton sternly, "The brains of the outfit."

Nate guffawed. Morgan giggled, at least in part because she had enjoyed his genuine snort of laughter so much.

Mrs. Wellhaven sent them a look, raised her baton and swung it down. The children watched her in silent awe. "That means begin!"

"She's a dragon," Nate whispered.

The children launched, a little unsteadily, into the opening number, "Angel Lost."

"What are you doing here?" Morgan whispered to Nate. "I thought you made it clear you weren't in favor of *The Christmas Angel*."

"Or shopping," he reminded her sourly. "I keep finding myself in these situations that I really don't want to be in."

"Don't say that like it's my fault!"

"Isn't it?"

She felt ruffled by the accusation, until she looked at him more closely and realized he was teasing her.

Something warm unfolded in her.

"I didn't know you were a carpenter, too," she said, trying to fight the desire to know everything about him. And losing.

He snorted. "I'm no carpenter, but I know my way around tools. I was raised with self-sufficiency. We never bought anything we could make ourselves when I was a kid. And we never hired anybody to do anything, either. What we needed we figured out how to make or we did without."

Though Morgan thought he had been talking very quietly, and she *loved* how much he had revealed about himself, Mrs. Wellhaven turned and gave them a quelling look.

Ace's voice rose, more croaky than usual, loudly enthusiastic, above her peers. "Lost annngelll, who will find you? Where arrrrre you—"

Mrs. Wellhaven's head swung back around. "You! Little redheaded girl! Could you sing just a little more quietly?"

"Is she insinuating Ace sounds bad?"

"I think she just wants all the kids to sing at approximately the same volume," Morgan offered.

"You're just being diplomatic," Nate whispered, listening. "Ace's singing is awful. Almost as bad as yours."

"Hers is not that bad, and neither is mine," Morgan protested.

"Hey, take it from a guy who spent an hour and a half with you oinking and braying, it is."

He was teasing her again. The warmth flooding her grew. "At least I gave you a break by sleeping all the way home."

"You snore, too."

Morgan's mouth fell open. "I don't!"

"How would you know?" he asked reasonably. "Snoring is one of those things you don't know about yourself. Other people have to tell you."

That seemed way too intimate—and embarrassing—a detail for him to know about her.

But when he grinned at her expression, she knew he was probably pulling her leg, and that he was enjoying teasing her as much as she was reluctantly enjoying being teased.

"Little redheaded girl—"

"Still, I'm going to have to go bean that shrew if she yells at Ace again."

"You." Mrs. Wellhaven rounded on him, and pointed her baton. "Who are you?"

"Little redheaded girl's father," he said evenly, dangerously, having gone from teasing Morgan to a warrior ready to defend his family in the blink of an eye.

Amazingly Mrs. Wellhaven was not intimidated. "No parents. Out. You, too, little redheaded girl's mother."

Morgan should point out she was the teacher, not a parent, certainly not a parent who had slept with this parent and produced a child, though the very thought made her go so weak in the knees, she had to reach out and balance herself by taking his arm.

Luckily, thanks to the darkening expression on Nate's face, she made it look as if she had just taken hold of him to lead him firmly out the door.

Touching him—her fingertips practically vibrating with awareness of how his skin felt—was probably not the best way to banish thoughts of how people produced children together.

Morgan let go as soon as they were safely out the auditorium door.

"She's a dragon," Nate proclaimed when the door slapped shut behind him. "I'm not sure I should leave Ace in there. Did you actually talk me out of taking my daughter to Disneyland to expose her to that?"

Morgan knew it would be a mistake to preen under his unconscious admission that she had somehow influenced him. Then again, she probably hadn't. He hadn't even noticed her hand on his arm, and her fingertips were still tingling! With the look on his face right now, he looked like the man least likely to be talked into anything.

Besides, between the look on his face—knight about to do battle with the dragon—and the attitude of Mrs. Wellhaven, she was getting a case of the giggles.

Nate eyed her narrowly.

"I don't get what's funny."

"If Mrs. Wellhaven is the brains of the outfit—" *and she couldn't even see that Nate was not a man to be messed with* "—the whole town is in big trouble."

Nate regarded her silently for a moment, and then he actually laughed.

It was the second time in a few short minutes that Morgan had heard him laugh. This time he made no attempt to stifle it, and it was a good sound, rich, deep and true. It was a sound that made her redefine, instantly, what sexy really was.

"It's not too late for me to go and bean her," he said finally.

"I'm afraid I don't even know what it means to 'bean' somebody."

He laughed again. "Morgan McGuire, I think you've led a sheltered life. Let's go grab a coffee. I can't listen to that." He cocked his head at the cacophony of sound coming out the door, and shook his head. Ace's voice rose louder than ever above all others. "Maybe I can still talk Ace into going to Disneyland."

"Maybe Mrs. Wellhaven will pay for you to go."

And then he laughed again, and so did she.

And she could feel that shared laughter building a tenuous bridge between them.

And so Morgan found herself in the tiny, mostly empty school cafeteria drinking stale coffee and realizing she was alone across the table from Nate Hathoway.

Without a forge as a distraction. Or Ace. Or even Old MacDonald.

They were not strangers. For heaven's sake, they had spent an entire day together! And yet Morgan felt awkwardly as if she didn't have one single thing to say to him. She felt like a sixteen-year-old on her first date. Nervous. Self-conscious. Worried about what to say. Or what not to say.

Be a teacher, she ordered herself. *Talk about Cecilia.*

But somehow she didn't want to. Not right this second. She didn't want to be a teacher, or talk about Cecilia. There was something about the pure *rush* of feeling sixteen again, tongue-tied in the presence of a gorgeous guy, that she wanted to relish even as she was guiltily aware it was the antithesis of everything she had tried to absorb while reading *Bliss*.

"So," he said, eyeing her over the top of the cup, "you get the coat hangers put up?"

"Thanks for the other pair. Two was plenty, but thanks. No, I didn't put them up. Not yet."

"Really? You don't like them?"

Oh, she liked them. Way too much. Liked caressing that smooth metal in her hands, liked the way something of him, his absolute strength and even his maddening rigidity, was represented in the work that he did.

"It's not that. I mean I tried to put them up. They keep falling down again. The first time it happened I thought I had a burglar. They're too heavy. I'm afraid they've made a mess of the wall."

He squinted at her. "You knew they had to be mounted on a stud, right?"

She willed herself not to blush, and not to choke on her coffee. He had not just said something dirty in the elementary-school cafeteria. She was pretty sure of it. Still, she couldn't trust herself to answer. She took a sudden interest in mopping a nonexistent dribble of coffee off the table.

"How long are the kids going to be singing?" he asked.

Thankfully, he'd left the topic of the stud behind him! "I was told the first rehearsal would be about an hour. I think that's a little long for six-year-olds, but—"

"The coffee's bad, anyway. You want to play hooky for a few minutes, Miss Schoolmarm?"

"Excuse me?"

He leaned across the table and looked at her so intently she thought she might faint.

"I'll show you what a stud is," he promised, his voice as sultry as a hot summer night.

"Pardon?" She gulped.

"You shouldn't go through life without knowing."

She felt as if she was strangling.

When she had nearly worn through the table scrubbing at the nonexistent spot, he said, "I'll hang up the coat hangers for you."

"You want to come to *my* house?"

He raised his eyebrows at her. "Unless you want the coat hangers hung somewhere else?"

"You want to come to my house now?"

His eyes had the most devilish little twinkle in them. "It's not as if you're entertaining a gentleman caller, Miss McGuire."

It was true. He was offering to do a chore for her. That involved *studs*.

She was not going to let him see how rattled she was! Well, he already had, but she intended to curb his enjoyment.

"Yes," she said, "that would be fine. A very gentlemanly offer from someone who is not a gentleman caller. Though I'm sure you are. A gentleman. Most of the time. When you aren't talking about beaning the choir director. Or hunting down the parents of children who have teased your daughter."

She was babbling. She clamped her mouth shut.

"Nobody's ever called me a gentleman before," he told her with wicked enjoyment.

But underneath the banter she heard something else. And so she said primly, "Well, it's about time they did."

Ten minutes later, she was so aware of how life could take unexpected turns. Just this morning it would have never occurred to her that Nate Hathoway would be in her house by this afternoon. In fact, Santa coming down the chimney would have seemed a more likely scenario.

And really, having Nate's handiwork in her house was a bad enough distraction. Now having him here, it seemed somehow her space was never going to be quite the same.

As if it would be missing *something*.

Stop it, Morgan ordered herself. She was *devoted* to independence. Nate showing her how to hang something without it falling back off the wall could only forward that cause!

That's why she had given in so easily to his suggestion to come over here.

Wasn't it?

No, said the little part of her that watched him filling her tiny space with his essence. There was an illusion of intimacy from having him in this space.

Now his presence was large as he loomed in her living room waiting for her to find a hammer.

When she came back from the basement with one, she found him eyeing her purple couch with a look that was a cross between amusement and bewilderment.

"Do you like it?" she asked, feeling ridiculously as if it was a *test*. Of course he wouldn't like it, proving to her the wisdom of living on her own, not having to consult with anyone else about her choices, proving the *bliss* of the single life.

"Yeah, I like it," he said slowly. "What I don't get is how a woman can make something like this work. If I bought a sofa this color it would look like I killed that purple dinosaur. You know the one? He dances. And sings. But it looks good in here. It suits you."

She tried not to show how pleased she was, his words so different from what she expected. "I call my decorating style Bohemian chic."

"You don't strike me as Bohemian," he said, looking at her thoughtfully. "I would think of that as kind of gypsylike. You seem, er, enormously conventional."

"Perhaps I have a hidden side," she said, a bit irked. Enormously conventional? That sounded boring!

"Perhaps you have. Perhaps you even have a hidden sheik," he said, "which, come to think of it, would be just as good as a hidden stud. Maybe better. What do I know?"

"C-h-i-c," she spelled out. "Not sheik!"

And then he laughed with such enjoyment at his own humor that she couldn't help but join in. It was a treat to hear him laugh. She suspected he had not for a long time.

She handed him her hammer.

He frowned, the laughter gone. "The couch is good. This? Are you kidding me? What is this? A toy?"

It occurred to her that a woman that linked her life with his would have to like a traditional setup. She would choose the furniture, he would choose the tools. She would cook the meals, he would mow the lawn.

Considering she had left her fiancé because he had taken what she considered to be a sexist view of her career aspirations, considering her devotion to the principles of *Bliss: The Extraordinary Joy of Being a Single Woman*, Morgan was amazed by how easily something in her capitulated to this new vision. How lovely would it be having someone to share responsibilities with?

Shared, maybe certain things would not feel like such onerous, unachievable chores. Could there be unexpected pleasures in little things like hanging a few coat hangers? Is that what a good marriage was about?

She didn't know. Her own parents had separated when she was young, her father had remarried and she had always felt outside the circle of his *new* family.

Her mother's assessment of the situation—that she was looking for her father—seemed way too harsh. But Morgan knew her childhood experiences had made her long for love.

Not just love, but for a traditional relationship, like the one her best friend's parents had enjoyed. How she had envied the stability of that home, the harmony there, the feeling of absolute security.

But after her relationship with Karl, its bitter ending, Morgan had decided the love she longed for was unrealistic, belonged in the fairy tales she so enjoyed reading to the children.

Now, with Nate Hathoway in her front entry, tapping her wall with her toy hammer, the choice Morgan had made to go it alone didn't feel the least bit blissful. It felt achingly empty. Achingly.

CHAPTER FOUR

NATE HADN'T REALLY expected Morgan's house to have this effect on him. It was cozy and cute, like a little nest. The enjoyment he had taken in her discomfort over agreeing to invite him over to help her find a "stud" was dissipating rapidly.

And who had pushed the envelope, who had suggested this foolishness? He wished he could blame her, but oh, no, it had been all him, lured by her blushing at the word *stud*.

Feeling the need to be a man, to do for her what she didn't have the skill to do herself.

But now, in her house, with her purple sofa and her toy hammer in his hand? It was his lack he was aware of, not hers.

This house made him feel lonely for soft things. Feminine touches, Cindy's warmth, seemed to be fading from his own house. The couch throw pillows she had chosen were worn out, the rag rug at the front door a little more rag than rug these days, the plaid blanket she had bought when Ace was a baby and that Ace still pulled over herself to watch television, was pathetically threadbare.

It reminded Nate, unhappily, how desperately inadequate he was to be raising a girl on his own.

What was it about Morgan that made him look at a life that he had felt he made full and satisfying despite the loss of his wife, to thinking maybe he wasn't doing nearly as well as he'd imagined? Around Morgan his life suddenly seemed to have glaringly empty spaces in it.

"Wow," he said, forcing himself to focus on her wall, to not give her even an inkling of the craving for softness that was going on inside of him, "for a little bit of a thing, you know how to destroy a wall."

"It wasn't intentional."

"Destruction rarely is."

He needed to remember that around Morgan McGuire. His life and Ace's had had enough unintentional destruction wrought on it. They could not bear more loss, either of them. He needed to do what he had come here to do, and get out, plain and simple.

Not that anything seemed simple with Morgan sharing the same room with him as it did when he brooded on it alone over the forge.

Nate brought himself back, shook his head again at the large holes where she had tried to hang his coat hooks and the weight of them had pulled chunks of drywall off the walls.

He tapped lightly on her entrance wall with a hammer.

"See? There's a stud." He glanced at her. She was refusing to blush this time, probably because of his explanation, so he went on explaining, as if his voice going on and on was an amulet against the spell of her. "You can hear the solid sound behind the wall. They're placed every sixteen inches. So you could put a coat hanger here, and—" he tapped the wall gently "—here. Here. Here."

"But that's not where I want the coat hangers," she said mutinously. "It's not centered properly. I want them in a row like this."

She went and took a pair of hangers from where he had set them on the floor, inserted herself between him and the wall and showed him.

"Here and here. And the other two in a straight line down from them."

He went very still. She was so close to him. He had no protection against this kind of spell. His craving for all things soft intensified. Her scent, clean, soap and shampoo, filled him. She was not quite touching him, but he could feel a delicate warmth radiating off her.

It seemed, dangerously, as if she could fill the *something missing* place in his life.

Nate knew he should back away from her a careful step but he didn't. He tried to hold up the amulet of words again. "Hmm. Guys don't think like that. For most men, it's all about function, not form."

But all the words did this time was make him more sharply aware of their differences, male and female, soft and hard, emotionally open and emotionally closed.

"Tell that to someone who hasn't seen your work," she said.

"I do try and marry form and function in my work."

Now his amulet, words, had come back to bite him. He contemplated his use of the word *marry* in such close proximity to her, hoped it was completely coincidental and not a subliminal longing.

He could not help but feel he was being drugged by her closeness, the spell of her winding its way around him, stronger than all that physical toughness he possessed.

Because Nate still had not moved. He could smell that good, good smell that was all hers. Wholesome. Unpretentious. But alluringly soft, feminine, just like this space.

She seemed to realize suddenly that she had placed herself in very close proximity to him.

She went as still as him, caught, too, in the unexpected bond of awareness that leaped sizzling in the air between them.

Then, stronger than him, after all, Morgan tried to slip away, back out under his arm, but he dropped it marginally, and they were locked together in the small space of the hallway.

He looked at her for a moment, the intensity between them as tangible as a static shock off a cat, or clothes out of the dryer. He was weakened enough. It was absolutely the wrong time to remember how soft her cheek had felt under his fingertips, and then his lips.

Nate was not seeing her as his daughter's teacher right now. Unless he was mistaken, her eyes were smoky with a longing that mirrored his own.

But he had already buried a wife. And his best friend. To believe in good things again felt as if it would challenge even his legendary strength.

Even this situation should be showing him something important. He had vowed he did not want to tangle any further with the young schoolteacher.

And yet, here he stood in her front hallway.

Nate knew, the hard way, that life could be wrested out of his control. His young wife had gone out the door, Christmas Eve, for *one more thing.*

One more thing for Ace's sock. He could even remember what it was, because she had told him as she went out the door laughing. *Reindeer poop.* Chocolate-covered raisins that one of the stores had bagged and labeled in tiny ziplock bags.

He'd been so glad to see her laughing, so happy to see her engrossed in getting ready for Christmas that he hadn't really paid any attention to the snow outside.

Why had he let her go? Why hadn't he offered to drive her?

And then, instead of Cindy coming back with reindeer poop, there had been that awful knock on the door, and a terrible descent into hell.

So, he knew, firsthand and the hard way, life could be snatched from your control.

It only made him more determined to control the things he could.

And he could still exercise some control over this. And he was aware that he needed to do it. The last thing he needed to do was give in to the insane desire to kiss Morgan again... And not on the cheek this time, either.

Congratulating himself on the return of his strength, feeling as Sampson must have done when his hair grew back and he pulled that building down, Nate dropped his arm, backed away. He needed to go *now*.

"Look, I'll make you a mounting board for the coat hangers. I've got some really nice barn wood at home that I'd been planning to reclaim. I'll fasten the board to the studs, so it's nice and solid, and then put the coat hangers on that." He looked at his watch. "Rehearsal is nearly over, Miss McGuire."

And he was aware as he said it that it could be taken a number of ways. That *their* rehearsal was nearly over. And what would that mean? The *real* thing to follow?

He hoped not, but now that he had promised her the barn board, he knew his escape was temporary. He was going to have to come back and put it up.

Hopefully he would have time to gird his loins against her before he did that!

They got back to the auditorium just as Mrs. Wellhaven was wrapping up. Ace flew off the stage and into his arms, seeming remarkably unscathed by her hour in the clutches of the dragon.

He lifted her up easily, and he felt the weight and responsibility of loving her, of protecting her from hurt, from more loss.

He glanced at Morgan over his daughter's head. His tangling with her teacher had the potential to hurt her. Bad.

"Guess what, Daddy?"

"What, sweetheart?"

"Mrs. Wellhaven says one of us, somebody from our class, is going to be the Christmas Angel! They get to stand on a special platform so it looks like they are on the top of the tree. They sing a song all by themselves!"

He knew this latest development had the potential to hurt Ace bad, too. His love for his daughter might blind him to her—like every father he thought his little girl was the most beautiful in the world—but he knew Ace's was not a traditional beauty. With her croaky voice and funny carrottop, she was hardly Christmas-angel material.

"She's letting all twenty-two of you think you have a chance of being the Christmas Angel?" He could hear annoyance in his voice, but Ace missed it.

"Not the boys, silly." She beamed at him. "Just the girls can be Christmas angels. It could be me!"

Ace's voice was even more croaky than ever, excitement and hope dancing across her very un-angel-like features.

Hope. Wasn't that the most dangerous thing of all?

Nate's eyes met Morgan's over the top of Ace's

head. She didn't even have the decency to look distressed, to clearly see how unrealistic his daughter's hopes were.

He felt the weight of wanting to protect his daughter from all of life's disappointments, felt the weight of his inability to do so.

"I should have beaned Mrs. Wellhaven while I had the chance," he said darkly. And he felt that even more strongly the next morning at breakfast.

"Daddy, I dreamed about Mommy last night."

Nate flinched, and then deliberately relaxed his shoulders. He was standing at the kitchen counter, making a packed lunch, his back to Ace, who was floating battle formations with the remains of the breakfast cereal in her bowl.

He knew his own dreams about his wife were never good. *Cindy swept away by a raging river, him reaching out but not being able to get to her. Cindy falling from an airplane, him reaching out the door, trying desperately to reach a hand that fell farther and farther away...*

He often woke himself up screaming Cindy's name.

Nate hadn't heard Ace scream last night. He tried not to let his dread show in his voice, but didn't turn around to look at her.

"Uh-huh?" He scowled at the lunch ingredients. If he sent peanut butter *again* was Morgan going to say something? When had he started to care what Morgan had to say?

Probably about the same time he'd been dumb enough to plant that impromptu kiss on her cheek.

It was ridiculous that a full-grown man, renowned for his toughness, legend even, was shirking from the judgments, plentiful as those were, of a grade-one teacher.

"It was a good dream," his daughter announced, and Nate felt relief shiver across his shoulder blades. Maybe finally, they had reached a turning point. Ace had had a good dream.

He recognized that he, too, seemed to be getting back into the flow of a life. If going shopping and volunteering to help with a town project counted. He suspected it did.

And did it all relate back to Morgan? Again, Nate suspected it did.

In defiance of that fact, and the fact that some part of him leaned toward *liking* Miss McGuire's approval, he slathered peanut butter on bread. Ace liked peanut butter. And she liked nonnutritiously *white* bread, too.

"You rebel, you," Nate chided himself drily, out loud.

"Do you want to hear about my dream?"

He turned from the counter, glanced at his daughter, frowned faintly. Ace was *glowing* in her new sparkle skinny jeans and Christmas sweater with a white, fluffy reindeer on it. Even her hair was tamed, carefully combed, flattened down with water.

He turned back to the counter. "Sure. Raspberry or strawberry?"

"Raspberry. In my dream, Mommy was an angel."

Something shivered along his spine. *You've been my angel, Hath, now I'll be yours.*

"She had on a long white dress, and she had big white wings made out of feathers. She took me on her lap, and she said she was sorry she had to leave me and that she loved me."

"That's nice, Ace. It really is."

"Mommy told me that she had to leave me right at Christmas because people have forgotten what Christmas is about, and that she was going to teach them. She said she's going to save Christmas. Do you think that's true, Daddy?"

After David had died, Cindy had found respite from her grief in that time of year. By the time Ace had come along, she *loved* every single thing about Christmas. Every single thing. Turkey. Trees. Carols. Gifts. *Reindeer poop.*

After David's death, she'd developed a simple faith that she had not had when they were children. Cindy believed God was looking after things, that there were reasons she could not understand, that He could make good come from bad.

While not quite sharing her beliefs, to Nate it had been a nice counterpoint toward his own tendency toward cynicism.

After she had died, his cynicism had hardened in him. In fact, he felt as if he shook his fist at the heavens. This was how her faith was rewarded? How could this have happened if things were really being looked after?

Show me the reason. Show me something good coming from this.

And the answer? Yawning emptiness.

He had buried her in the gravesite in an empty plot that was right beside David. Nate had gone to that gravesite a few times, hoping to feel something there. A presence, a sense of something watching over him, but no, more yawning emptiness.

So his cynicism hardened like concrete setting up on a hot day, and he didn't go to the graveyard anymore, not even when Cindy's sister, Molly, went to mark special occasions, birthdays, Christmas.

And now listening to Ace chatter about angels,

it felt as if his cynicism had just ramped up another gear.

Why did he have an ugly feeling he knew exactly where this was going?

"I hope so, honey." Because, despite the cynicism, he was aware nobody needed Christmas saved more than him and his daughter.

Unfortunately, he was pretty damned sure Ace's dream had a whole lot more to do with Mrs. Wellhaven's ill-conceived announcement about one of Ace's class being chosen the Christmas Angel than with her mother.

Ace confirmed his ugly feeling by announcing, sunnily, "In the dream, Mommy told me I'm going to be the Christmas Angel!"

Nate struggled not to let the cynicism show in his face. Still, he shot a worried look at his daughter.

Even with the new clothes and better hair, Ace looked least likely to be the Christmas Angel, at least not in the typical sense he thought of Christmas angels: blond ringlets, china-blue eyes, porcelain skin.

Ace looked more like a leprechaun, or a yard gnome, than an angel.

"Poor Brenda," Ace continued. "She thinks it's going to be her. I wonder if she'll still be my friend if it's me."

Brenda Weston, naturally, took after her mother, Ashley, and looked like everyone's vision of the Christmas Angel. Chances were she didn't sing flat, either.

"You know it was just a dream, don't you, Ace?"

"Mrs. McGuire says dreams come true."

Thank you, Miss McGuire. There she was again, somehow front and center in his life.

"Miss McGuire," he said, choosing his words with great care, "doesn't mean dreams you have while you're sleeping come true. She means dreams you think of while you're awake. Like you might dream of being a doctor someday. Or a teacher. Or a pilot. And that can come true."

"Oh, like stupid Freddy Campbell thinks he's going to be a hockey player?"

"Exactly like that."

"Can he?"

"I don't know. I guess if he works hard enough and has some natural talent, maybe he could."

Ace snorted. "If Freddy Campbell can be a hockey player, I can be the Christmas Angel. See? I'm dreaming it while I'm awake, too."

There was no gentle way to put this.

"Ace, don't get your hopes up." He said it sternly.

She smiled at him, easily forgiving of the fact he was doing his best to dash her dreams. "Don't worry, Daddy, I won't."

"You know what?" he said gruffly. "You're the smartest kid I ever met." Six going on thirty. Maybe that wasn't such a good thing, but Ace beamed at him as if he'd presented her with a new puppy.

"The Christmas Angel probably has to be smart," she decided happily.

He sighed. Over the next few days, he'd try and get it through to her. She wasn't going to be the Christmas Angel. And he'd better let Morgan know he didn't want this particular brand of hopeless optimism encouraged.

An excuse to talk to Morgan, a little voice inside him, disturbingly gleeful, pointed out.

He had to deliver her the board he'd made for her coat hangers anyway. So, maybe he'd kill two birds with one stone. And then he'd be out of excuses for seeing her.

And *then* he'd get back on track in terms of distancing himself from her, protecting his daughter and himself from the loss of coming to care too deeply for someone.

Which meant he knew the potential was there. That Morgan McGuire was a person you could come to care too deeply about if you weren't really, really careful.

"Come on, squirt, I'll drive you to school." He shoved Ace's lunch into a bag, and went to the table. He roughed her hair, and she got up and threw her arms around his waist, hugged hard.

"I love you, Daddy."

And for one split second, everything in his

world seemed okay, and Ace, the one who had given him a reason to live, seemed like the most likely angel of all.

Morgan's doorbell rang just as the Christmas tree fell over. Thankfully it made a whooshing sound, probably because it was so large, so she heard it and leaped out of the way, narrowly missing being hit by it.

"Hell and damnation!" she said, regarding the tree lying in a pool of bent branches and dead needles on her floor.

Her bell rang again, and Morgan climbed over the tree that blocked her entrance hallway and went and flung open the front door.

Nate Hathoway stood there, looking like damnation itself. Despite the cold out, he wore a black leather jacket and jeans. Whiskers darkened his cheeks. His eyes sparked with a light that would have put the devil himself to shame.

"I thought you were opposed to cussing," he said mildly, white puffs of vapor forming as his hot breath hit the cold air.

Silently, she *cussed* the lack of insulation in her old house that had allowed her voice to carry right through the door. She also cussed the fact that she was wearing a horrible pair of gray sweatpants and a sweatshirt that said Teachers Spell It Out.

While she was on an inward cussing spree, Morgan also cursed the fact that she could imagine, all too well, what the slide of that warm breath across her neck would feel like.

"I am opposed to cursing in front of children!" she defended herself. "In cases of duress, amongst consenting adults, it's fine."

His eyes narrowed with fiendish delight. She wished she would have chosen a term different from consenting adults. It was a mark of how flustered his unexpected appearance had made her feel that she had said that!

And it was obvious he was thinking that phrase usually referred to something quite a bit more exciting than cussing.

"What was the crashing noise?" he asked, peering over her shoulder.

"Nothing!" she said stubbornly. It was her first Christmas by herself. She had never set up a tree before. Frankly, it was one of the loneliest and most frustrating experiences of her single life. And she wasn't pretending otherwise because Amelia Ainsworthy, someone she did not know, and was not likely to meet, thought such efforts at aloneness were character building!

He glanced behind her. The tree was lying there, blocking the door.

"Did your tree fall down?"

He did *not* sound gentle. Did he? Maybe he did, a little bit. But it didn't matter!

"I set it there," she lied, hoping to hide both her loneliness and her frustration from him. "It's too tall. I'm going to put the lights on before I stand it up."

"Don't take up poker," he advised her solemnly. "You made that decision after it fell, didn't you?"

She shrugged, trying not to let on how his appearance had made her aware of a dreadful weakness in her character. Morgan *wanted* a big, strong guy just to come in and take over.

She wanted a man to figure out the blasted stand, saw off those bottom branches, muscle the huge, unwieldy tree into place, put the star on top and figure out lights that looked as if they required a degree in engineering to sort out.

Nate truly was the devil, arriving here at a horrible moment, when she felt vulnerable and lonely. He was tempting her to rely on something—or *someone*—other than herself. She was sending him back into the night.

"Do you want help with the tree?"

"No," she spat out quickly before the *yes, yes, yes* clawing its way up her throat could jump out and betray her.

He nodded, but he could clearly see the horrible truth. She was the kind of helpless female the new her was determined not to have any use for!

"I brought over the board to put the coat hangers on. I could put it up for you if you want."

Her eyes went to what he was holding. A

helpless female might weep at the beauty of the board he had reclaimed for her. It was honey-colored, the grains of the wood glorious, the surface and edges sanded to buttery smoothness.

Well, right after he put it up for her, she was sending him back into the night. She would draw the line at allowing him to help with the tree.

Despite wanting to rebel against the teachings of the blissfully single Amelia, Morgan knew she would be a better person, in the long run, if she put that tree up herself. She stepped back from the door, and he stepped in.

She touched the board. "That's not what I was expecting," she said. "Something worn and weathered. When you said it was barn wood, I thought gray."

"It was, before I ran it through the plainer. Some of this old wood is amazing. This piece came from a barn they pulled down last year that was a hundred and ten years old." His fingers caressed the wood, too. "Solid oak, as strong and as beautiful as the day they first milled it."

Morgan was struck again by something about

Nate. His work always seemed to be about things that *lasted*. There was something ruggedly appealing about that in a world devoted to disposable everything.

Including relationships.

There was a tingle on the back of her neck. A relationship with this man would be as solid as he was, a forever thing, or nothing at all.

Don't you dare think of him in terms of a relationship, the devoted-to-independence woman inside her cried. But it was too late. That particular horse was already out of the barn.

"Where's Ace?" she said, glancing behind him.

"The Westons took her to the Santa Claus parade and then she's sleeping over at their place. Ace is thrilled."

As she closed the door, she read a moment of unguarded doubt on his face. "You, not so much?"

"I don't know. I don't quite get the purpose of it. I get going tobogganing, or to a movie. I don't get sleeping at someone else's house."

Don't blush, she ordered herself. They were not talking about *adult* sleepovers.

"Sleeping is not an activity," he muttered.

"Believe me, they won't be doing much sleeping. Probably movies and popcorn. Maybe some makeup."

"Makeup?" He ran a hand through his hair and looked distressed. "I hoped I was years away from makeup. And don't even mention the word *bra* to me."

Believe me, that was the last word I was going to mention to you.

He could fluster her in a hair, damn him. She tried not to let it show. "Not serious makeup. Not yet. You know, dress-up stuff. Big hats, an old string of pearls, some high heels."

"Oh."

"Is there something deeper going on with you?" she asked. "Something that needs to be addressed?"

Morgan saw she could fluster him in a hair, too.

"Such as?" he asked defensively.

"Any chance you don't like losing control, Nate?"

He scowled, and for a moment she thought she was going to get the lecture about knowing everything again. But then she realized he wasn't scowling *at* her. After a long silence, he finally answered.

"I don't know what I'm supposed to do," he admitted reluctantly. "I felt like I wanted to call the Westons and conduct an interview."

Interrogation, she guessed wryly. "What kind of interview?"

"You know."

She raised her eyebrows at him. He sighed. "Just casually ferret out information about their suitability to have Ace over. Don't you think I should know if anyone in the house has a criminal record? Don't you think I should know if they consume alcoholic beverages? And how many, how often? Don't you think I should know if they have the Playboy channel? And if it's blocked?"

Morgan was trying not to laugh, but he didn't notice.

"Even if I got all the right answers," he continued, "I still would want to invite myself over and just as casually check their house for hazards."

"Hazards? Like what?"

"You know."

"I'm afraid I can't even imagine what kind of hazards might exist at the Westons' house."

His scowl deepened. "Like loaded weapons, dogs that bite, unplugged smoke detectors."

She was biting the inside of her cheek to keep from laughing. She knew it would be the wrong time to laugh. "The Westons are very nice people," she said reassuringly. "Ashley is active in the PTA."

He sighed. "Intellectually, I know that. That's how I stopped myself from phoning or going in. I grew up with Ashley Weston. Moore, back then. She was a goody-goody. I guess if Ace has to sleep somewhere other than her own bed, I want it to be at a house where I know the mom is a goody-goody. Sheesh. The PTA. I should have guessed."

"Don't knock it until you try it," Morgan suggested drily.

"I'm not trying it. Don't even think about sending me a note."

There were quite a few single moms in the PTA, probably the same ones who swarmed him at the supermarket, so, no, she wouldn't send him a note.

"Still—" he moved on from the PTA issue as if it hardly merited discussion "—what about next time? What if Ace gets invited to someone's house where I didn't grow up with their parents? Or worse, what if I did, and I remember the mom was a wild thing who chugged hard lemonade and swam naked at the Old Sawmill Pond? Then what?"

No wonder he had an aversion to doing his grocery shopping locally. That was way too much to know about people!

"I'm not sure," she admitted.

"Oh, great. Thanks a lot, Miss McGuire! When

I really want an answer, you don't have one. What good is a know-it-all without an answer?"

Morgan was amazingly unoffended. In fact, she felt she could see this man as clearly as she had ever seen him. She suddenly saw he was *restless*. And irritable. He had needed to do something tonight to offset this loss of control.

"Is this the first night you've been apart since the accident that took her mom?" she asked softly.

He stared at her. For a moment he looked as though he would turn and walk away rather than reveal something so achingly vulnerable about himself.

But then instead of walking away, he nodded, once, curtly.

And she stepped back over the fallen tree, motioning for him to follow her, inviting him in.

Morgan knew it was crazy to be this foolishly happy that he had picked her to come to, crazier yet that she was unable to resist his need.

But how could anyone, even someone totally emancipated, be hard-hearted enough to send a

man back into the night who had come shoulder-
ing the weight of terrible burdens? Not that he
necessarily knew how heavy his burdens were.

He hesitated, like an animal who paused, sens-
ing danger. And what would be more dangerous
to him than someone seeing past that hard exterior to his heart?

And then, like that same animal catching the
scent of something irresistible, he moved slowly
forward. He stepped over her tree, and she wondered if he knew how momentous his decision
was.

If he did, he was allowing himself to be distracted. He surveyed the strings of lights strewn
around her living room floor, the boxes of
baubles, the unhung socks. For a moment it
looked as if he might run from the magnitude
of what he had gotten himself into.

But then he crouched and looked at the tree
stand, a flying-saucer-type apparatus, that was
still attached solidly to the trunk of the tree. It
just hadn't kept the tree solidly attached to the
floor.

"Is this what you expected to hold your tree?" he asked incredulously.

It was the kind of question that didn't really merit an answer. Though it had been the most expensive tree stand at Finnegan's, a tree nearly crashing down on top of her was ample evidence that the design was somewhat flawed.

"It's worse than your hammer," Nate decided, with a solemn shake of his head. Still, he looked pleased that he had found something in such dire need of his immediate attention.

"I bought a new hammer," she said.

After his last visit, she had decided she wasn't having her hammer choice keep her from the promised bliss of the single woman.

Though somehow, in this moment, Morgan knew she had missed the point because she felt ridiculously eager to show it to him, secretly, weakly wanted his approval of her choice.

"Really?" But he hardly seemed interested in her new acquisition of a hammer. He had already moved on to other things.

With raw strength that made her shiver, he

yanked the stand off the trunk of the tree and scowled at it, looked at it from one way and then another.

"I think I can fix it." He began to whistle through his teeth, a song that sounded suspiciously like "Angel Lost" though she decided against pointing that out to him, because he was so obviously pleased to have things to look after since Ace was out of his reach for the evening.

Morgan told herself she was duty bound to resist this beautiful gift of a man coming to help her. Duty bound.

So, naturally she didn't.

"I'll go make cocoa," she said, and then, in case that might be interpreted as far too traditional, she let the independent and blissful woman speak up, too. "And I'll get my new hammer, too."

CHAPTER FIVE

"THIS IS YOUR HAMMER?" he asked. Nate tried not to laugh. Good grief. She was an all-or-nothing kind of girl. She had gone from the toy tapping tool that had looked more like an instrument her first graders would use in a percussion band, to this, a 23-ounce Blue Max framing hammer with a curved handle. It looked like a hatchet.

"What's wrong with it?" Morgan asked.

"Nothing."

"It was very expensive."

"I'm sure it was. I'll bet that tree stand was, too."

"Don't take that 'there's a sucker born every minute' tone with me."

"Yes, ma'am," he answered her schoolmarm tone of voice.

But she wasn't fooled. Not even a little bit. "You think my new hammer is funny. I can tell."

It probably wasn't a good thing that she was getting so good at reading him.

"No, no, it's not funny." Despite saying that a snort of laughter escaped him. And then another. Then he couldn't resist. "When are you building a house?"

"A house?" she asked, flabbergasted.

And he dissolved into laughter. He had not laughed, it seemed, for a very long time. Oh, little chuckles had been taking him by surprise here and there. But it had not been like this. A from the belly, caught in the moment, delight-filled roar of genuine laughter.

It felt good to laugh again. Maybe too good. It almost made him forget he had other worries tonight, like Ace and her new little pal, who could at this moment be gooping on makeup, or eating popcorn in front of an unblocked Playboy channel.

"A big hammer is called a framing hammer. It's used for framing a house."

"I'm sure it can be used for other things."

"Yeah. If you can lift it. And swing it. Have you seen house framers? They have wrists nearly as big as your thighs."

Shoot. Was she going to guess he'd been looking at her thighs? Maybe not, because she suddenly seemed distracted by his wrists. She licked her lips. He decided it might be best to avoid mentioning body parts from now on.

Or looking at them. For a prim little schoolteacher, she had lips that practically begged to be kissed, full and plump.

He wasn't going to be held responsible for what happened next if she licked them again.

"You don't buy a hammer you can barely heft," he said, a little more sharply than he intended. His sharpness had nothing to do with her hammer choice, not that she ever had to know.

She reacted to the tone, which was so much better than lip-licking. Rather than looking educated, she looked annoyed. Annoyance was good!

"I like that hammer," she said stubbornly.

"Really?" he challenged her. "What do you like about it?"

She hesitated. She looked at the hammer. She looked at him. She looked at her toes. And the fallen Christmas tree. It was written all over her that she wanted to lie, and that she was incapable of it.

"The color," she finally admitted, giving him a look that dared him to laugh. It was a look designed to intimidate six-year-old boys and it was effective, too.

Or would have been effective if she hadn't started laughing first. He liked it that she could laugh at herself, and then they were both laughing. Laughing with her, for the second time in just a few minutes, was a worse temptation than sneaking peeks at how those prison-issue sweatpants hugged her thighs.

Because it invited him back toward the Light. Nate was aware he was walking way too close to the fire.

He reined himself in. "I'll just put up the coat hangers now," he said. To himself he added that he would put up the coat hangers—that was what he had come here to do—and go. Immediately.

"Show me how to do it," she said, setting down the cocoa she had brought in. "Next time I need something done, you might not be here."

Not *might not,* he corrected her silently. *Won't.* A week ago, he would have said it out loud… Why not now? Because, despite his vow to stay away, he kept coming back to her, magnet to steel.

Because there was something about her that was funny and sweet and even a hard man such as himself could not bring himself to hurt her by tossing out carelessly cruel words.

"Come on then," he said gruffly. "I'll show you."

It was a surrender. Because putting up a few coat hangers should have been the simplest thing in the world. It should have taken five minutes.

Instead, because of his surrender, half an hour later the reclaimed barn board was finally up. His hand had brushed her hand half a dozen times. Their shoulders had touched. He was aware of her lips and her thighs and her shoulders and her scent.

He was amazed he'd managed to get that board level, the coat hooks spaced out evenly.

Morgan was glowing as if she'd designed a rocket that could go to Mars as she surveyed their handiwork.

"It looks so good."

"Except for the additional hole," he pointed out wryly. She had put the huge hammer through the drywall when she had missed the nail he was trying to teach her to drive.

He had supplies to fix it, since he'd come prepared to fix her previous holes in the wall. He taped the hole, stirred the drywall mud and began to patch.

"I want you to promise you'll return the hammer." Then, he heard himself promising that if she did, he'd help her pick out one that was better for all-around household use and repairs.

Even though he knew darn well Harvey could help her. Harvey had been handling the hardware department at Finnegan's since time began. Nate could even go in and warn him to offer her a little advice on her purchases, before he actually let her buy them.

Whether she wanted it or not.

But she probably wouldn't, and for some reason he thought she might listen to him a little more than she would listen to Harvey.

Thought that meant something.

She was coming to trust him.

Oh, Nate, he told himself, cut this off, short and sweet. Wouldn't that be best for both of them?

"The cocoa's gone cold," she said, oblivious to his inner war. She took a little sip and wrinkled her nose in the cutest way. A little sliver of foam clung to the fullness of her lip. "I'll go make some more. Let's take a break."

Which meant she thought he was staying, and somehow, probably because of the damn foam on her lip, he could feel short-and-sweet going right out the window.

Well, Nate rationalized, he couldn't very well leave her with her Christmas tree sprawled across the floor, with a stand that was never going to stand up, could he?

Yes.

But he'd said he'd fix it.

He trailed her to the kitchen and watched her make cocoa. Since she was going to the effort, he'd drink that. Then he was leaving, tree or no tree. He had a kid he hired to help him sometimes, he'd send him over tomorrow. He could look after having it fixed without fixing it himself. But then would it be done right?

Her kitchen, like her living room, made him aware of some as yet unnamed lack in himself.

Everything was tidy, there was not a single crumb on the counter, no spills making smoke come off the burners as she heated the milk. She reached for a spice and the spices were in a stainless-steel container that turned, not lined up on top of the stove. The oven mitts weren't stained and didn't have holes burned in them.

He could feel that horrible *longing* welling up in him.

Leave, he told himself. Instead of leaving as

completely as he would have liked, he left the kitchen and went and worked on the stand. So it would be done right.

By the time she came back in, he had the stand modified to actually hold up a tree, and had the tree standing back up.

"This is a foolishly large tree," he told her.

She smiled, mistaking it for a compliment. "Isn't it?"

He sighed. "Where do you want it?"

"I should put the lights on while it's on the ground," she told him. "Come have your cocoa before it cools this time. I'll worry about the tree later."

But somehow, he knew now he'd be putting the lights on it for her, too. It was too pathetic to think of her trying to put them on with the tree lying on the floor, creative as that solution might be to her vertical challenges.

It occurred to him, she was proving a hard woman to get away from. And that with every second he stayed it was going to get harder, not easier.

Okay. The lights. That was absolutely it. Then he was leaving.

He went and sat beside her on the couch as she handed him cocoa. He took a sip. It was not powdered hot chocolate out of a tin, like he made for Ace on occasion. It was some kind of ambrosia. There was cinnamon mixed with the chocolate.

Morgan McGuire had witch-green eyes. She was probably casting a spell on him.

"So, do you and Ace have family to spend the holidays with?" she asked.

He wished he would have stuck with the lights. That was definitely a "getting to know you" kind of question.

"We alternate years. Last year we were with my parents, who live in Florida now, so this year we're with Cindy's side of the family, Ace's aunt Molly and uncle Keith. They have a little place outside of town. We'll go out there after the production on Christmas Eve and spend the night."

He didn't say his own house was too painful a

place to be on Christmas Eve. He did not think he could be there without hearing the knock on the door, opening it expecting to see Cindy so loaded down she couldn't open the door.

By then, Cindy had been gone so long he suspected she was coming home with a little more than reindeer poop.

"How about you?" he asked, mostly to avoid the way his thoughts were going, to deflect any more questions about his plans for Christmas.

Which were basically *get through it.*

She was the kind of woman you could just spill your guts to. If you were that kind of guy.

Which he wasn't.

"Oh." She suddenly looked uncomfortable. "I'm not sure yet."

"You won't go home?" he asked, suddenly aware it wasn't all about *him*, detecting something in her that was guarded. Or maybe even a little sad.

"No," she said bravely. "With *The Christmas Angel* on Christmas Eve I decided to just stay here."

Again, focused intently on her now, he heard something else. And for whatever reason, he probed it.

"Your family will be disappointed not to have you, won't they?"

She shrugged with elaborate casualness. "I think my mom is having a midlife crises. After twenty-three years of working in an insurance office, she chucked everything, packed a backpack and went to Thailand. She told me she'll be on a beach in Phuket on Christmas day."

"And what about your dad?"

"He and my mom split when I was eleven. He's remarried and has a young family. I'm never quite sure where I fit into all that." And then she added ruefully, "Neither is he."

Nate didn't know what to say.

His family might have been rough around the edges, but not knowing where you fit into the arrangement? He had been alternating where he spent Christmas since he had married Cindy and his mother still cried when it wasn't her year to have him and Ace.

The idea of your own family not wanting you was foreign to him. He felt so shocked and saddened by it, he had to fight back an urge to scoop her up and take her on his lap and rock her, like the lonely child he heard in her voice.

"It's actually been good," she rushed on bravely. "I'm doing all these things for the first time by myself. Before my mom decided to be a world traveler, she always *did* Christmas. And she was elaborate about it. Theme trees. New recipes for stuffing. Winning the block decorating party. Christmas was always completely done for me. In fact, God forbid you should touch anything. Then it might not look perfect. So, I don't know how to do anything, but I'm happy to learn. You don't want to go through life not knowing how to do things like that. For yourself."

She was not a very good liar. She was not *happy* to learn. But he went along with her.

"No," he said soothingly, without an ounce of conviction, "you don't."

"Of course, I probably won't cook a turkey," she said. "For myself. That would be silly."

"You aren't going to be alone on Christmas." He wasn't quite sure why he said it like that. As if he knew she wasn't going to be alone at Christmas. When he didn't. At all.

She was silent. Too silent.

He shot her a look. Her face was scrunched up, and not in the cute way it had been when the chocolate had gone cold.

"Are you going to cry?" he asked with soft desperation.

"I certainly hope not."

"Me, too."

He fought again that impulse, to pick her up and lift her onto his lap, to pull her head against his shoulder and hold her tight.

Instead, and it was bad enough, he reached out and took her hand in his, and held it. It was a small gesture. Tiny against the magnitude of her pain.

Nothing, really.

And yet something huge at the same time. She clung to his hand as if he had tossed her a life preserver.

That should have been enough to make him let go. But it wasn't. He was leaving his hand there as long as she needed to hold it.

Nate understood instantly that something had shifted in him. He had come out of the cave of his pain just enough to reach out to someone else.

A shaft of light pierced the darkness he had lived in.

And he saw the truth: all evening the dark place had called him to come back. And he almost had obeyed that call.

There was something comforting and familiar about that place of pain where he had been. Save for Ace, it made few demands on him. He did not have to feel anything, he did not have to truly engage with life. It certainly did not ask him to grow or to *give*.

But now, now that that shaft of light had pierced him, he was not sure he could go back to living in darkness. He was not sure at all.

Morgan took a deep shuddering breath.

"Let's put up the lights on the tree," he

suggested. If there was one thing personal pain had taught him, it was that sitting around contemplating it was no way to make it go away. Action was the remedy.

"Okay," she said, her voice wobbly with the tears she had not shed. She let go of his hand abruptly and leaped to her feet. "I guess that means I have to find the star."

Nate noted that everything she owned was brand-new, and there was a sadness in that in itself.

His childhood might have been poor, but both sides of his family had given him Christmas relics that went on his tree every year. He was pretty sure his lights, the color cracked off them in spots, predated his birth by several years. He had antique ornaments that his grandmother had carried across the ocean with her, acorn ornaments that Cindy had made when she was Ace's age.

Morgan's lack of anything old in her Christmas decoration boxes made him acutely aware of how bad her first Christmas alone could be.

And it was that awareness—of her aloneness, of how close to tears she had been—that made him tease her.

About the size of her tree, and the rather large size of the striped sock she put on the mantel for herself, about her selection of treetop star, a gaudy creation of pink-and-green neon lights.

He teased her until she was breathless with laughter, until the last remnants of sadness had left her face, and the sparkle in her eyes was not from tears. He was heartened when she began teasing him back.

Together, they put up the lights, ornaments way too scanty for such a big tree, tons of tinsel that she demanded, in her schoolteacher voice, get added to the tree a single strand at a time.

By the time they were done, it was close to midnight.

She insisted on making more hot chocolate. She turned off all the other lights in her house, and they sat on her purple couch in darkness made happy by the glow of the Christmas tree lights.

Nate had not realized how on guard he was against life, until now, when his guard came down.

He felt as relaxed as he had felt in years. And exhausted. Keeping a guard up that high was hard work he realized, it required constant vigilance.

And that was the last thing he thought.

He was still sitting up, but Nate Hathoway had gone to sleep on her couch, Morgan noted. Another woman might have thought it wasn't a very exciting end to what had turned out to be a wonderful evening.

But, staring at him mesmerized, Morgan thought it was perfect.

Sometime during the night—around the time she had made that announcement about spending Christmas alone, intended to solidify in her own mind and his her independence, but somehow turning pathetically maudlin instead—he had let go of some finely held tension in him.

Now, she loved watching him sleep. She could

study him to her heart's content without the embarrassment of him knowing.

And so she indulged in the guilty pleasure of just looking at him: the crumple of dark hair against his collar, the lashes so thick they could have been ink-encrusted, and cast soft shadows that contrasted the hard angles of his face, cheekbones, nose, chin.

His jaw was relaxed. And he didn't snore.

Sighing with the oddest contentment, she got up, finally, moved the hot chocolate from where he had set it on the ottoman and unplugged the Christmas lights. She fetched a blanket.

Her intention was to toss it lightly over him and tuck it around him.

But his head was tilted at an odd angle, so she gently leaned over and put pressure on his shoulder. He sighed, leaned, and she tucked a pillow behind his head.

Better, except that she felt reluctant to remove her hand from his shoulder.

He reached up and took her wrist, yanked gently. "Lie down beside me."

She knew he was sleeping, or in that groggy state between being asleep and being awake where he didn't really even know who she was or what he was asking.

His guard had come way down tonight. Now he was in a really vulnerable state, admitting something he would probably not normally admit.

He did not want to be alone.

Just like her.

She knew she should disengage his fingers one by one from her wrist and tiptoe off to her own room. Probably he would wake sometime in the night, be embarrassed to find himself asleep on her couch and disappear.

So she knew what she *should* do. But it seemed all her life had been about *shoulds*. The one time she'd rebelled and not put her own life on hold because she *should* defer to her fiancé's more lucrative career it had ended rather badly.

So, maybe she'd become even more attached to shoulds than before.

For all its talk of the joy of freedom, wasn't *Bliss: The Extraordinary Joy of Being a Single*

Woman just another book of shoulds? It was a desperate need for an instruction manual to guide her through life, to make the rules for her. Hadn't the book just provided another excuse not to rely on herself, *not* to risk following her instincts, *not* to risk taking control of her own life?

This was the truth: there was no instruction manual for life.

No one was going to grade her on what she did next. It was possible no one even cared. Her mother was in Thailand. Her father had long ago replaced his first family.

So why not do what she truly wanted? Why not do what would give her a moment's pleasure, even if that pleasure was stolen?

She didn't have to *stay* tucked into Nate's side. She could just see what it felt like, enjoy it for a few minutes and then go to bed.

With a sigh of pure surrender, Morgan sat on the edge of the couch, leaned tentatively into him. He was so solid it was like leaning against a stone, except the stone was deliciously sun-warmed.

He let go of her wrist, but his arm, freed, circled her waist and pulled her deep into his long leanness. For a moment, she felt as if she couldn't breathe.

What was she going to say if he woke up suddenly and completely?

She held her breath, waiting, but he didn't wake up. If anything his breathing deepened, touched the sensitive skin of her ear, felt on her neck exactly as she had always known it would, heated, as textured as silk.

She willed herself to relax, and as she did, she noticed her awareness of him deepening. Her own heart seemed to rise and fall with his each breath. He was not all hard lines as she had first thought. No, he radiated warmth, and his skin, taut over muscle, bone, sinew, had the faintest seductive give to it.

There, she told herself, she had felt it. She could get up and go to her own bed now, satisfied that she had followed her own instincts.

Except it was harder than she could have imagined to get up, to leave the warmth and strength of him, to walk to her lonely room and her cold bed.

It was harder than she could have ever imagined to walk away from what was unfolding inside of her. A brand-new experience. A very physical feeling of connection. Closeness. Awareness.

A physical experience that had a mental component…

For as she snuggled more deeply into him, Morgan felt the moment begin to shine as if it had a life of its own.

Her mind struggled to put a label on the level of sensation she was experiencing. And then it succeeded.

Bliss.

Morgan fell asleep in the circle of his arms. And woke in the morning to winter sunshine pouring through her windows.

For a moment, she felt it again, *bliss.*

But then she realized why she had awoken. It was because he was awake. Oh, God. Why hadn't she just enjoyed the sensation for a moment and then gone to bed as she had originally planned?

It would have saved them both the terrible embarrassment of this situation.

Now it felt horribly awkward. He hadn't even been fully awake—maybe not even partially awake—when his hand had encircled her wrist and he had asked her to lie down with him.

What was he going to say now?

What the hell do you think you're doing?

Morgan could feel her whole body stiffening, bracing itself for his rejection.

Instead, his fingertips brushed her cheek.

"Hey," he said softly, something of discovery in his voice, "you have a print on your cheek again."

He didn't kiss it this time, though, just put her away from him, got to his feet and stretched.

The rumpled T-shirt lifted as he stretched his arms over his head, showing her the taut washboard of his stomach.

Her gaze drifted upward to his face. He was

smiling. He didn't seem to find the situation awkward or embarrassing at all.

"Hmm," he said thoughtfully, "I guess now I
know what's so great about sleepovers."

He was not sorry. It occurred to her that he
hadn't been asleep at all when he'd invited her
to cuddle with him. It hadn't been an accident.
Or a case of groggy mistaken identity.

"Is my hair standing straight up?" she asked
him.

He cocked his head. "No. More sideways."

That's what *wasn't* so great about sleepovers.
And what now? Did she offer him breakfast? Did
she show him the door?

He had his cell phone out of his pocket,
scrolling through it. "No calls from Ace," he
said with relief.

It was the mark of what kind of man he was
that Morgan had not even known he had a cell
phone until that moment.

Karl's had been more than a cell phone: it
could practically start his car on command, and

she realized now that Karl's cell phone had been like a third party in their relationship.

And that it would never be like that with Nate Hathoway.

"But I think I better go get her. Saturday is *our* day. She's pretty fussy about that."

"Okay." Was she being dismissed? That made her feel so bereft she couldn't even tease him about not going shopping this time.

"You want to spend our day with us?"

Her mouth fell open.

"I promised Ace a sleigh ride."

A sleigh ride?

She had to say no. Look at how she had just spilled the beans to him last night about her whole life history! Look how she had reacted when she thought she was not going to be included in his plans for the day!

Bereft.

No, throwing out the rule book did not mean leaving herself wide-open to hurt. And to get involved with this man had the potential to make her redefine *hurt*.

On the other hand, a sleigh ride?

Morgan nearly sighed out loud. It was the kind of family outing her childhood dreams had been full of. Despite her mother creating a picture of a perfect Christmas, there had never been the connection of a perfect Christmas. Christmas activities had involved *entertaining,* not playing.

Morgan had dreamed of tobogganing and skating and sleigh rides. She had dreamed it in such perfect detail that she could picture it already, with startling clarity. The three of them—her, Nate, Ace—nestled in a sleek red sleigh, their legs covered in a soft, plaid blanket.

He would be holding the reins of a spirited white stallion. The horse would snort, throw up clouds of snow with each prancing footfall. The air would be full of diamond ice crystals and the sound of bells.

There was an old-fashioned romance about his invitation that was irresistible.

"I'd love to join you and Ace on a sleigh ride," Morgan said.

Even though it was against her better judgment,

this thing was unfurling inside her, like a flag. More than happiness. More than excitement. More than anticipation.

This time it was familiar to her, so Morgan identified it much more quickly.

"Happy," Nate said.

She preened that he had recognized her mood so quickly.

"That's Ace's pony's name. It's kind of like when people name a Great Dane Tiny. He's not that great with a sleigh."

Okay, so he hadn't recognized her mood. And the white steed was out. Still, gliding across snow-covered fields was gliding across snow-covered fields.

"I'll come back for you in an hour or so," he promised.

And he was gone, which was good, because she had been gravely tempted to lean forward, close her eyes and offer her lips as a form of goodbye.

"You're dreaming," she warned herself as she heard his vehicle roar to life outside.

In fact, it would have been too easy to dismiss the whole thing as a dream, except that her coat hangers were hung and her Christmas tree was up. Except lights winked from the branches, and the star, that age-old symbol of hope, shone bright from the very top of that tree, a pinnacle she could not have reached without a ladder.

It would be easy to dismiss the whole thing as a dream, except that when Morgan looked in the mirror, her hair was standing up sideways and her cheek held the perfect imprint of his shirt.

CHAPTER SIX

"MRS. MCGUIRE, this is Happy." Ace patted the Shetland pony vigorously, kissed his nose. Ace's lips were stained an unnatural shade of red as if she had smeared them with raspberries.

"You were right about the lipstick," Nate had told Morgan, rolling his eyes, when they had picked her up.

"And you were wrong about—"

"Everything," he admitted. "No hazards of any kind. Don't ask me to admit I was wrong ever again. It unmans me."

He was teasing her, and Morgan was coming to enjoy the growing ease between them so much. But she liked the underlying message, too. That somehow their lives were linked, and *ever again* suggested it might be staying that way.

Even this outing suggested that. By inviting her

to this Christmas-card-pretty farm—red barn, snow-covered fields, cows behind white fences— that belonged to his and Ace's family, weren't the links that connected them growing stronger?

Now Nate was trying to get a harness on the uncooperative, chunky brown-and-white pony. So far his hand had been stepped on twice. He had said something—both times—quite a bit stronger than "damn," then shot Morgan looks that dared comment.

But she did not want to be the schoolteacher today. Just a woman enjoying the extraordinary bliss of not being alone, of sharing a wonderful winter day with a glorious man and his adorable little girl.

"This is the meanest horse ever born," Nate grumbled. "Keep your face away from his teeth, for God's sake, Ace. He might mistake your lips for an apple."

"He loves me," Ace said with certainty. "He won't bite me."

"I don't know why he doesn't bite her," Nate told Morgan, apparently not convinced it was love. "He's bitten me at least six times since our unhappy first meeting. Mostly, now I can manage to outwit him."

"But not the time he bit you on the bum," Ace said. "Remember, Daddy?"

"Speaking of being unmanned," he muttered with a sigh. "That's kind of a hard one to forget. I couldn't sit down for a week."

She shouted with laughter.

The sleigh ride might not be turning out quite as she'd expected, but Morgan loved the feeling growing inside her. It was blissful. She didn't just feel as if she was being included in this little family outing. She felt as if she belonged.

If she contemplated it, she might find it just a little bit frightening that she was feeling something right now, in this very moment, that she had been waiting her whole life to feel.

But she determined not to contemplate it, not to wreck these precious moments by trying to look into that foggy place that was the future. For once, she would just enjoy what she had been given, no worrying, no analyzing, no planning, no plotting.

"He's going to be good today," Ace predicted. "Be good, Happy."

"Ace thinks he's going to pull the sleigh. I think he won't. Unless there's a cliff nearby that he can pull us all off."

"I don't think horses are that...devious, are they?" Morgan asked. The stocky miniature steed trying to sidestep the traces was so different from the stallion of her imagination she laughed out loud again.

Or maybe the laughter had nothing to do with the surprise of the pony. It was the day. And being with him. Them. The very air seemed to be tingling with merriment, with joy.

Snow was beginning to fall gently. The little horse stamped his feet and shook his mane, and a lovely smell drifted up from him. In the background was a redbrick farmhouse, snow drifts in the front yard, a cheery wreath on the front door.

Ace had told her that was her aunt Molly's

house, and that she wasn't home right now. Happy had been her Christmas gift from her aunt last year.

Morgan thought it took a pretty special aunt to know what a hard time Christmas would be for this child, and to come up with a gift good enough to make a dent in all that sadness.

In fact mischief and merriment seemed to dance in the air around the pony. Finally, Nate loaded her and Ace into a red sleigh. The pony did have bells on, and as it set off, their music filled the air.

And that was about the only part of Morgan's fantasy that had been realistic. Nate wasn't even cuddled under a blanket with her and Ace. He walked to one side of the pony, trying to persuade him to keep up a forward motion.

An hour later, Morgan thought she had never laughed so hard in her entire life. She was doubled over she was laughing so hard.

"You have to stop," Morgan gasped. She was begging.

"We are stopped," Nate pointed out, not sharing

her amusement. "That's the problem. Unhappy hasn't moved for ten minutes."

It was snowing, but it was no longer big, gentle flakes floating down around them. It was coming down hard now, the wind whipping it up in gusts around the sleigh. But even the freezing cold could not dampen Morgan's enjoyment.

Nate stood in front of Happy, pulling on the pony's obstinate head, trying to get him to move.

The pony had pulled the little sleigh, with Ace and Morgan in it, only in stops and starts, mostly stops. Ace held the reins, and jiggled them and shouted encouragement, while her father walked slightly behind and to the right of the pony.

Forward movement was accomplished sporadically when Nate slapped the pony's ample brown-and-white rump with his gloves.

Now, a mile from the house, Happy was no longer startled by the rather frequent popping across his rump with the gloves. Apparently he had decided against forward motion and was not going to be persuaded with glove smacks.

"I think he likes it," Morgan said, watching the pony sway his rump happily into the pressure of Nate's hand after every increasingly vigorous smack with the gloves. Happy turned his head just enough that she could see the pony's decidedly beady eyes half shut in an expression that Morgan had to assume was pure pleasure.

Nate had his hands firmly planted on either side of the pony's headstall and was leaning back hard on his heels, pulling with all his might.

"Come on, you dastardly little devil."

Considerable as Nate's might was, the pony outweighed him by several hundred pounds. Happy planted his own feet, and showed Nate he wasn't the only one who could lean back!

"There's a dog-food factory waiting for you!" Nate warned the pony darkly. "One phone call. The meat wagon comes by here on Monday."

"Please stop," Morgan begged again. All this cold, all this jolting and all this laughter was having the most unfortunate effect on her kidneys.

"He's just kidding," Ace whispered. "He says that every time."

The pony stepped back instead of forward, pulling Nate with him.

"On second thought, dog food is too good for you," Nate muttered. "Bear bait. The bear-bait wagon comes by on Wednesday."

The pony cocked his head, as if he was actually considering this, then stepped back again, yanking Nate backward with him.

"Please," Morgan moaned.

"It's time for the apple," Ace yelled. If she was enjoying her sleigh ride any less for its lack of forward movement it didn't show in her shining face.

"I am not bribing him to move. I'm just not. It's a matter of pride with me. Hathoways are renowned for their pride, Morgan."

But after another few minutes of unsuccessfully playing tug-of-war with the four-hundred-pound pony, Nate sighed and produced an apple, apparently kept on hand for just this purpose.

With a sigh of resignation, he held it at arm's

length. Happy opened one eye, caught sight of the apple and lurched forward.

A terrible move for a suffering kidney.

"Greedy little pig," Nate muttered, keeping the apple carefully out of the snapping pony's reach and breaking into a jog.

Morgan howled with laughter as the fat pony stirred himself into a trot, stretching his neck hard to get the apple. The sleigh jolted along behind him, as Nate wisely looped back toward the barn while the pony was moving!

They finally got back to the barn, Happy's only true ambition demonstrated when that building came back into view and he broke into a clumsy gallop that had Nate running to keep up.

"Give him the apple, Daddy," Ace insisted when they arrived at the barn door.

Panting, Nate obliged, yanking back his fingers when Happy tried to devour them along with the apple.

Morgan decided then and there you could learn a lot about the true nature of a man from how he bargained with a pony—and from the lengths he was willing to go to make his daughter happy.

Nate helped Morgan out of the sled with a rueful grin. He gave a little bow. "I see I have entertained you." And then more solemnly revealed, looking at her so intently her face burned, "I like it when you laugh, Morgan McGuire."

"I like it, too."

"I'm sure that this was not exactly what you pictured when I promised you a sleigh ride."

"The truth?" she said. "It's not. And it was so much better! Except for one thing." She leaned forward and whispered her urgent need to him.

"Ace? Take Miss McGuire up to the house."

The door of the farmhouse opened just as they arrived. An attractive wholesome-looking woman with dark hair and a Christmas sweater smiled her welcome at them.

"Aunt Molly!" Ace cried.

"You must be frozen," Molly said, as she gave Ace a huge hug.

"Actually," Morgan said awkwardly, "if you could point me in the direction of—"

Thankfully she didn't even have to finish the sentence, because Molly laughed. "Right there. I've jounced around in that sled, too."

When Morgan joined them again, Molly explained she had been out Christmas shopping when they arrived.

"How was Happy today?" she asked her niece.

"Happy was extra bad for Daddy today," Ace declared gleefully.

"Oh, good," Molly said, and they all shared a laugh that made Morgan feel, again, that deepening sense of family, of being part of a sacred circle. She had a sense of ease with Molly that usually she would not have with a person quite so quickly.

"I'm Morgan McGuire, Ace's teacher," Morgan said, extending her hand.

"Oh, the famous Mrs. McGuire."

"It's Miss. I can't get that through to the kids. I've stopped trying."

"Miss. Oh," Molly said, and she turned and looked down to where Nate was taking the harness off the pony. Her eyes went back to Morgan full of soft question.

Questions that Morgan was thankful had not been spoken out loud, because she would have had no idea how to answer them.

There was something happening between her and Nate, there was no question about that. But it was ill-defined and nebulous. Were they becoming friends? Morgan thought it was something more. Possibly a lot more. But did he?

"Ace's mom, Nate's wife, Cindy, was my sister," Molly said, leading Morgan through to the kitchen.

It could have been an awkward moment, but it wasn't.

Molly laid her hand on Morgan's. "We love him very much. We just want him back. Sometimes," she mused, sighing, "I feel as if I lost all three of them."

"Three?" Morgan said.

"Never mind. It's a long story. And maybe it will have a happy ending someday. I could have sworn when I looked out the kitchen window a few minutes ago, I saw Nate smiling. A rare enough occurrence in the last two years, and even rarer after he's had to deal with the pony!

"Oh. Here's Keith, my husband. Keith, this is Morgan. Nate brought her out to have a sleigh ride with Ace."

No mention of her true role in their lives, as Ace's teacher.

"And how was that?" Keith asked her.

"One of the most deliriously delightful experiences of my life."

He watched her for a moment, and like his wife, seemed satisfied.

Silly, to be so pleased that Nate's family by marriage liked her. They hardly knew her.

Though that seemed to be a circumstance they were determined to change, because after Nate came in, stomping the snow off his boots, they were all invited to share the pot of chili that had been heating on the stove.

"Morgan?" Nate asked. "Does that fit with your schedule?"

Schedule? Oh, a woman more clever than her

would probably at least pretend to be busy on a Saturday night. But somehow, there was no way you could play games with a man as real as Nate.

Or not mind games. Not flirting games. Other games? He proved to be enormously good at them.

Because after the feed of chili in the warmth of the kitchen, with banter going back and forth between the two men, there was just an expectation they would stay. The kitchen table was cleared of dishes and a worn deck of cards came out.

They taught her to play a game called 99 that she was hopeless at. But two late night's in a row soon proved too much for Ace, and despite her winning streak at 99 she finally went and laid down on the couch and fell asleep.

And then the adults gathered around the fireplace, and Molly made hot rum toddies, though Nate refused and had hot chocolate instead.

Morgan wished she had refused, too. The drink filled her with a sense of warmth and well-being as the talk flowed around her. About the farm and the forge, the coming production of *The Christmas Angel.*

"Did you hear they were deciding who gets to go by a lottery system?" Molly asked.

Morgan confirmed that. There were only three hundred seats available in the auditorium, so the seats would be given away by a lottery system. But she told them that there would be a live feed to the community center and one of the local churches so that everyone who wanted could see it.

"And have they chosen the Christmas Angel yet?" Molly said, casting a worried look at her sleeping niece. "She's called me several times about it. Tonight's the first night I haven't heard her mention it."

"I understand Mr. Wellhaven will announce the choice at his welcome party. It's a skating party at the pond, a week from tonight. He's been sent video of some of the rehearsals."

"I'd like it to be over with," Molly said.

"Me, too," Nate said. "I hate to think how disappointed she's going to be."

"Who knows?" Morgan said. "Maybe she won't be disappointed. Maybe it will be her."

Molly's and Nate's mouths fell open in equal expressions of shocked disbelief.

"Ace?" they said together.

"I've told all the girls they have an equal chance of being chosen."

"But that's not true," Nate said grimly. "Ace can't sing a note, and she doesn't look like anyone's idea of an angel."

"Her singing has actually improved quite a lot under Mrs. Wellhaven's tutelage."

"She sings all those songs around the house all the time. I haven't noticed any improvement."

"Well," Morgan said firmly, "there has been. And I think anyone with a little imagination could see she would make a perfectly adorable Christmas Angel."

"I don't want her getting her hopes up for something that doesn't have a snowball's chance in hell of happening."

It was the first grim note in a perfect day, so Molly quickly changed the subject, but the mood had shifted.

A few minutes later, saying goodbye on the doorstep, Nate cradling the sleeping child against his chest, it seemed to Morgan as if she had never had a more perfect day. She realized it was not the toddy alone that allowed her to feel this sense of warmth and well-being. It had only allowed her to relax into the feeling instead of analyzing it.

"Nate," she said, as they drove through the snow, "it's so nice that you still are so connected with them, with Cindy's family."

He shot her a surprised look. "Family is family. They became my family the day I married Cindy."

Morgan shivered. She had always known he was a *forever* kind of man. Not like in her own family, where loyalties shifted with each new liaison. She could feel herself longing for what he represented.

Morgan realized tonight had been the kind of night she had always dreamed of.

A simple night of family. And connection. A feeling of some things not being temporary.

"I still think it's nice," she said.

"We had already lost Cindy. It would have just made everything so much worse if we lost each other. Ace is what remains, she's what Cindy is sending forward into the future. I could never keep her from her aunt, from her mom's sister."

But Morgan thought of all the people—including her own family—that when something happened, like a divorce, that's exactly what they did.

"When my mom and dad divorced," she told him, "it was like my dad's whole side of the family, including him, just faded away."

"You didn't have any contact with your dad?"

"A bit, at first. Then he moved for a job, and then he remarried. So, it was a card and some money on my birthday. He always paid my mother support, though."

"Yippee for him," Nate said darkly. "There's a lot more to being a dad than paying the bills."

"Yes," she said. "I can see that in the way you parent."

"Now you like my parenting?" he teased her. "What about the notes?"

"You haven't gotten one for a while!"

"I kind of miss them."

"You do not."

They were in front of her house now, but he made no move to get out of the truck. "What your dad did? That was wrong," he said, after a long time. "And sad."

She liked that about Nate Hathoway. He had a strong value system. He knew what was right and what was wrong, and he would never compromise that.

"Nate, tell me if it's none of my business, but did someone else die, besides your wife? Molly said something."

For a long moment he didn't answer. Then he said gruffly, "There were three of us who grew up together. Me, Cindy and David. Cindy and

David had been in love since they were about twelve. I mean really in love. The head-over-heels kind. Some people outgrow things like that, other people don't. They didn't."

He was silent for a long, long time. "David joined the army. Before he left he made me promise I'd look after her. If anything happened."

"Something happened," Morgan guessed when he was silent for a long time again.

He cast her a look that said it all, that confirmed that strong value system.

"David was killed in Iraq," he said roughly. "And I looked after Cindy, just like I promised."

She wanted to ask if he loved her, but it was so evident from the agony on his face that he had loved her. Loved both his friends.

"You are a good man," she whispered. She wanted to ask, *Did she love you? The really-in-love kind? The head-over-heels kind?* But she could tell by the set of his face he already felt he might have said too much.

He shrugged it off uncomfortably, and they

pulled up to her house. He shut off the truck, and leaped out, not wanting to discuss it anymore. Still, he walked her up to her front door, helped her with the key.

"Thank you, Nate," she said softly. "It was such a perfect day."

"You're welcome." He turned to go down off her stoop.

Maybe it was the hot rum toddy.

Or maybe it wasn't. Maybe it was that he was a good, good man, who had made a vow to his best friend and kept it. Maybe it was because she thought he deserved to be *really* in love and suspected that he had sacrificed that feeling in the name of honor.

"Nate?"

He turned back to her.

Something else had been between them all day, too.

Awareness.

She crossed the small distance between them, stood on tiptoes and did what she had wanted to do from the moment she had met him.

She tasted him. She touched her lips to his own.

He tasted exactly as she had known he would.

Of mysterious things that made a woman's heart race, but underneath that, of strength and solidness. Of a man who would do the right thing.

Of things made to last forever.

She stumbled back from him, both frightened and intrigued by the strength of her longing.

He was a man, she knew, who had been tremendously hurt.

She held her breath knowing that everything between them had just shifted with the invitation of her lips.

So far everything had been casual and spontaneous.

Now their kiss changed that.

It asked for more. It demanded some definition, it asked where things were going. It asked if he was ready to *really* fall in love.

The head-over-heels kind.

Because despite it all, despite her determination

to be independent, to not give her life away, she felt ready to surrender to the tug inside her.

To love him.

Morgan held her breath, thinking he would walk away, perhaps never to look back.

But he didn't. He regarded her solemnly, and then said, softly, "Wow."

Then he walked away, leaving her feeling as if things were even more up in the air and ill-defined than they had been before.

"Mr. Hathoway?"

Nate glanced at the clock. It was just a little after 7 a.m. Morgan must have assumed he was up getting Ace ready for school. The truth was he had the process down to a science. He could get her ready, including hair, breakfast and bag lunch in under fifteen minutes.

"Yes, Miss McGuire?" he asked. Nate hadn't called her since the sleigh ride, since her unexpected kiss and the clear invitation in it.

He hadn't called her because he had told her things he had not expected to tell her. She was proving she could take chinks out of armor that not a single other person had even dented.

But Morgan McGuire wanted things that Nate could not promise. After that night with Molly and Keith, playing games, laughing, everything easy and light, he was aware of a deep longing in him, too.

To have a life like the one he'd had before. A stable life, where you woke up in the morning and trusted the day would go as you planned.

The truth? He wasn't even sure he could be the man he had been before, a man naively unaware how quickly things could go wrong in the world, naively believing his strength would be enough to protect those he loved from harm.

He was aware how vulnerable answering a longing like that made a man.

"I'd like to discuss my last note with you."

But here was another truth. Despite his desire to harden himself against Morgan McGuire, her temptations and invitations, he could feel a smile starting somewhere in the vicinity of his chest. He relished it, that he was lying in bed under the warmth of his blanket, the phone to his ear, listening to her.

He relished when she used that snippy, schoolmarm tone of voice on him. He wondered when that had happened, exactly, that he had started enjoying that schoolmarm tone.

"I sent you a request to send cookies for Mr. Wellhaven's welcome party at the skating rink at Old Sawmill Pond."

"I sent the damned cookies."

Silence. "We've discussed cussing."

"Ace is still in bed."

He could tell she was debating asking how he could get her ready for school in time if she was still in bed, but she wisely decided to stick to one topic at a time.

"All right," Morgan said, after a pause. "Let's discuss the damned cookies, then."

The smile was turning to laughter. He bit it back.

"I'm in charge of cookies for the welcome party for Mr. Wellhaven. He'll be arriving Saturday."

"The note said that." Plus, Ace was in excitement

overdrive about the skating party to be held at the pond in Mr. Wellhaven's honor. Nate was going to have to give her the gift he had planned to give his daughter from Santa—the new skates—early.

"You said you missed my notes," she pointed out.

"Hmm," he returned, noncommittally. "I did say that." He realized what he missed was her.

"After she received my note, Mrs. Weston sent four dozen sugar cookies decorated individually like gift-wrapped Christmas parcels."

"Good for Ashley."

"Mrs. Campbell sent three dozen chocolate-dipped snowmen. Sharon McKinley sent melt-in-your-mouth shortbread, shaped like Christmas balls, with icing ribbons."

"How did you know they were melt-in-your-mouth? Are you sampling the cookies, Miss McGuire? Tut-tut." He heard her bite back laughter.

Why were the simplest things such a joy with her?

"Mrs. Bonnabell sent—"

"Look, it sounds like you have plenty of cookies. You won't even need the box of Peek Freans I sent over."

"That is hardly the point, Mr. Hathoway."

"What is the point?"

"Everyone else made the effort."

"Fine. I'll ask Molly to whip me up a batch of brown snowmen, with ribbons around their necks, holding Christmas parcels. Individually decorated."

"Your listening skills are very good, Mr. Hathoway."

"Thank you." Ridiculous to feel pleased that she had noticed how closely he listened to her every word. *However,* he guessed.

"However," Morgan continued, "I don't really think it's fair to ask Molly to contribute to *our* class project."

"I don't know how to make cookies."

"Well, yes, I understand that. It is a situation that can be remedied. I mean, a few short weeks ago, I didn't know how to hang a coat hanger."

"You're not exactly ready to start building furniture."

"No, I suppose not."

Said a bit doubtfully, as if she might actually
be considering trying to build some furniture.
He reminded himself he'd have to follow up on
getting her a new hammer before she wrecked
something else trying to use the one she had.

"The point is," Morgan said, "I was willing to
learn. If you and Ace would like to come over
this afternoon after school, I would be happy to
teach you how to make Christmas cookies."

His schedule had become insane because of
the volunteer hours he was putting in on the set
of *The Christmas Angel*. He still had special
orders he had to get out for Christmas, as well
as the gate commission.

Plus, he was avoiding Morgan. And her lips.
And the clear invitation he had seen in her eyes
the other night after the disastrous sleigh ride.
Boy, if a sleigh ride like that couldn't scare a
girl off, what would?

And there was the other disastrous thing, too. Telling her about Cindy and David had poked a little hole in the dam of feelings walled up within him… He was all too aware that he might be like the little boy hoping his finger poked in that hole was going to be enough to hold it back.

The thing was, her voice on the other end of the phone was like a lifeline thrown to a man who had been in the water so long he didn't even know he was drowning.

The thing was, he knew it had cost her to make the move, and he could not bear to hurt her. It seemed she had experienced quite enough hurt in her life. Not at the hands of fate, either, but at the hands of the very people who should have loved and protected her.

Though there was probably a far more sensible way of looking at that. Hurt her a little now. Or a lot later.

He didn't feel like being sensible. Or maybe, closer to the truth, he was not as sure as he had been a few weeks ago about what sensible was.

"Sure," he said, as if he grabbed lifelines every single day. "What time would you like us to come make cookies?"

CHAPTER SEVEN

As it turned out, after school, Ace had been offered a Christmas shopping outing to Greenville with the Westons. She still had to buy something for her daddy, she informed Nate, and it would be much too hard to keep it a secret if he came with her.

She was so excited about going shopping with her new friend Brenda that he didn't have the heart to tell her she would be missing making cookies with her teacher. Having to make such a momentous choice would have torn her in two.

Nate knew he could phone and cancel, and maybe even *should* phone and cancel, but as he moved up the walkway to Morgan's house, he contemplated the fact that he hadn't.

And knew he was saying yes to the Light.

Even though he knew better. Even though he

knew, better than most, life could be hard, and cruel, and made no promises.

When Morgan opened her door, that's what he saw in her face. Light. And he moved toward it like a man who had been away for a long time, a soldier away at the wars, who had spotted the light pouring out the window of home.

An hour later her kitchen was covered in flour and red food coloring. He was pretty sure there were more sprinkles on the floor than on the cookies.

And, despite the fact she was the world's best teacher, calm, patient, clear about each step and the order to do them in, those cookies were extra ugly. Sugar cookies, they were supposed to look like Christmas tree decorations. They didn't.

He held one of the finished cookies up for her. "What does this look like?"

She studied it. "An icicle?"

"Morgan, it looks like something obscene." He bit into it, loving her blush. "But it tastes not bad."

She put her hands on her hips, still very

much Miss McGuire, pretending that kiss of a few nights ago wasn't hanging in the air between them like mistletoe, pretending her face wasn't on fire. "Has anyone ever told you you're incorrigible?"

"Of course," he said, picked up a misshapen Santa and bit his head off. "That's part of being a Hathoway."

"Really?" She surveyed the cookies, apparently realized they were not going anywhere near Wesley's welcome party, picked one up and bit into it. "Tell me about growing up a Hathoway."

And oddly enough, he did. In Morgan's kitchen, surrounded by the scent of cookies baking and a feeling of *home,* Nate told her about how it was to grow up poor in a small town.

"But," he said, making sure she knew he was not inviting pity, "we might have been poor, but our family was everything. We were fiercely loyal to each other. My dad couldn't give my mom much materially, but I don't think a man has ever loved a woman the way he loves her.

He would fight off tigers for her. For any of us. There was an intense feeling of family.

"And we might have been poor, but we were never bored." He told her about working in the forge since he was just a little boy, starting on small chores, working up to bending the iron.

He told her about making their own fun, since they could never afford anything. In the summer fun was a secondhand bicycle and the swimming hole, or a hose and a pile of dirt.

"You haven't really lived until you've squished mud through your toes," he told her. "And in winter fun was a skate on a frozen pond in skates way too big because they were purchased to last a few seasons. It was tobogganing on a home-made sled, and snowball fights. It was an old deck of worn-out cards in the kitchen."

"Like at Molly and Keith's the other night?" she said, and he heard the wistfulness.

"Yeah, growing up was like that…" Each of his memories held Cindy and David. It was the first time in a long time he felt the richness of that friendship, instead of the loss. It was the first time he understood how much it had become a part of who he was today.

"Tell me about how you grew up," he invited Morgan.

And then Morgan told him about her family, and how fragmented it was, how some of her earliest memories were of tension, of feeling as if she was responsible for holding something together that could not be held.

"It was like trying to stop an avalanche that had already broken free," Morgan said. "My mom and dad eventually split when I was eleven. And it was a blessing, but it made me long for things I couldn't have."

"Such as?"

She smiled sadly. "I used to watch other families on the block, families on television, and long for that. To be together with other people who loved you in a special way. A way that both shut out the rest of the world, and made you able to go into it in a different way."

He was astonished how sad he felt for her. "I'm

surprised you don't have it, if you longed for it," he said gruffly.

"I tried to set it up, to manipulate it into happening, to impose my sugarplums-and-fairies vision of family on every single relationship I was in, but I just ended up more disillusioned. At some point, I decided the kids I taught would be my family."

It seemed to him that this was a lesson Morgan would teach him again and again. It wasn't all about him. Maybe that was part of the legacy his two best friends had left him with.

When you cared about people, putting what they needed sometimes came ahead of what you needed.

He knew he wasn't a man who could be counted on to make anyone's life better forever. Certainly he could not be trusted with sugarplum-and-fairy fantasies about family.

But he could probably be trusted with making her feel better for one single day.

And that day was today.

"Eating all these cookies?" he said.

"Yes?"

"Has made me really hungry. Want to go for Chinese?"

Taking somebody for Chinese food was a sign of a serious relationship in a small town, but she probably didn't know that.

She smiled at him, and he was bathed in the light of that smile.

"Yes," she breathed as if something was settled between them. So, maybe she knew what going for Chinese in small towns meant after all.

And really over the next few hectic days, it felt as if something *was* settled between them. Whatever it had been in Nate that could fight her, and his attraction to her, could fight no more.

The rehearsals were stepped up now in preparation for Wesley Wellhaven's arrival. The children were practicing their parts in earnest, and Mrs. Wellhaven still frowned on an audience, so more and more Nate and Morgan used that as an excuse to slip away.

They were not dates. Or at least Nate told himself they were not dates.

Because mostly they were mere moments stolen from crowded schedules.

A quick walk around the block the school was on. A cup of coffee in the cafeteria. A shared crossword puzzle and biscotti at Bookworms café down the street. Sometimes, they'd sit in his truck, the heater blasting, just talking or sharing a newspaper. Once they had a snowball fight in the parking lot.

There was a time when all this waiting for Ace to finish rehearsals would have grated on Nate. Now he looked forward to every minute he got to spend with his daughter's teacher.

When he was with Morgan, Nate had the strangest sensation that he was discovering the town he had always lived in as if it was brand-new to him.

He had never ridden the horse-drawn wagon that old Pete Smith drove around town for the three weeks before Christmas. Now he did. He had never taken the Light Tour, following a map through the town of the best Christmas deco-rated properties, but one night, when the kids were in a late rehearsal, he and Morgan did that. He had never been in Canterbury Tails, the pet store, but one time they went in and played on the floor with the new golden-retriever puppies that would be ready to go home for Christmas. Morgan guided him through the foreign land of the antiques stores and the bookstores and the art galleries. He'd lived in Canterbury his whole life, and he saw its museum for the first time with her at his side.

Morgan's sense of wonder, her joy in discovery, was obviously part of what made her a teacher her students adored. But it was also what gave Nate the sensation that it was all brand-new, an adventure that had always been right in front of him all his life but that he had missed completely.

His own sense of wonder, his joy in discovery, seemed to be all about her. More and more her hand found its way to his, and he savored the feeling of it: soft and small within his larger one.

He kissed her. At first lightly, casually, but as time went on, the kisses deepened, and instead of slaking some desire inside of him the taste of her fueled it.

Nate found himself telling Morgan things he had never told another person, and she told him things he suspected she had never told another person.

Nate began to feel things around Morgan that he had never felt. He would never say it was a better relationship than what he had had with his wife.

But it was different.

He and Cindy had grown up together, he had known her forever. He had loved her, and he had loved David, and when the time came he had kept his vow to David gladly.

But now, with Morgan, sometimes Nate would remember Cindy's words to him, a long time ago.

I wish you could know what it is to fall in love, Nate.

Stop it, Cin, I love you.

No. Head over heels, I can't breathe, think, function. That kind of fall-in-love.

At the time, he had thought she was crazy. He hadn't felt he could love anybody any more than he loved her.

But now, with Morgan, he saw that there were different kinds of love. It felt as if Cindy's wish for him was coming true.

You've been my angel, Hath. Now I'll be yours.

For the most pragmatic man in the world to even consider those words and wonder if they could be true was a measure of what was happening to him.

Nate felt as if he was making a choice, saying yes to something that was bigger than him. He had never felt like this: breathless with wanting, on fire with life and longing.

The simplest things: discussing the newspaper, opening a fortune cookie at a Chinese-food restaurant, playing with a puppy on the floor, it all made him feel so intensely alive, almost as if he had sleepwalked his way through life, and now the touch of her lips, her eyes on his, her hand folded into his hand, were making him come fully gloriously awake.

He was aware of feeling like a teenage boy around Morgan, wanting to show off for her. He loved how he could make her eyes catch on his muscles when he flexed, how his breath would stop in his chest when she caught the tip of that little pink tongue between her teeth.

He loved the stolen kisses, the sizzling moments of pure awareness, the desire building to heat that could melt steel. He loved the smoky look that would cloud her green eyes after they kissed.

And he loved it that they didn't give in, as he had with Cindy. That they let the *wanting* become a part of the tantalizing sizzle of being together.

He felt dazzled, as if he was conducting an old-fashioned courtship, as if he had become the gentleman she had promised him she could see, even when no one else ever had.

When Nate was not with Morgan it felt as if the color had leeched from his world, as surely as the color leeched from the autumn leaves, stealing their reds and golds and oranges until they were just brown.

He anticipated seeing her. He found himself thinking of little ways to win that smile. He sent her a single orchid in a candleholder. He made her little trinkets at the forge, a frog, a chunky bracelet, a set of little metal worry beads.

Morgan's relationship with Ace was a marvel. She knew everything there was to know about little girls. She knew about hair bows and pink shoes and underwear with the days of the week embroidered on each pair. She knew about doll's clothes, and Hannah Montana and baking things.

His little girl was blossoming like a cactus that had waited for Christmas.

But through it all, Nate felt as if he was in a love-hate relationship with himself, as if his surrender to all these good things and good feelings was temporary.

He liked the way it felt to be excited about life, to explore the mysteries and gift of another human being. But at the same time he hated the sensation of losing control.

The feeling of *choosing* this was leaving him. Because with every day that Morgan's laughter and her nearness filled his life with light, it felt the choice to walk away was a door that was closing.

What man could choose to go back to darkness after he had been in the Light?

Maybe walking a great distance in darkness was even about this: recognizing the Light when you felt it. Honoring it by knowing it was something not to be taken for granted.

Nate was beginning to see the events of his life in a larger perspective.

How would you even know it *was* light, if you had never known darkness?

He was so accustomed to being a man of action that these thoughts, deep and complex, troubled him.

And it troubled him even more when he realized what was happening.

He could call it whatever he wanted: discovering

the Light, learning to play again, having fun, being awake.

But all those names could not really distance him from the truth that it was far deeper than any of the labels he was trying to attach to it.

Nate knew it when he found himself in Greenville, alone, *shopping,* a weekday when both Morgan and Ace were at school.

The thing was, he knew darn well he had not come here to shop for Ace. No, Ace's parcels were spilling out from under their Christmas tree in a pile so high and wide they were taking over the living room.

No, Nate had taken advantage of the fact Morgan and Ace were in school to make the trip to Greenville by himself to find something to give Morgan for Christmas.

He wasn't quite sure what. The hammer in the bag from the building supply store—a nice little 12-ounce curved-claw trim hammer—didn't quite cut it.

He wanted something that would let her know what she had come to mean to him. He wanted something so special. Something spectacular. And yet subtle at the same time.

Something that would make that light come on in her face, the one that he was starting to live for.

Something…but what?

Everything he looked at seemed wrong. Gloves? Ridiculously impersonal. Hat and scarf? Too generic. Books? Too stuffy. Lingerie? Not nearly stuffy enough.

He found himself standing at the window of Orchid Jewelers in the mall he had never once been to before he met Morgan.

Maybe, he found himself thinking, *I should just make her something at the forge.*

Around him was the bustle of shoppers, the tinkle of bells, carolers, the ho-ho-ho of the mall Santa.

All these things—the noises, the colors, the decorations, the music, the good cheer—all these things a mere year ago would have made him cringe.

He could feel the healing happening in the fact

he felt the Christmas excitement, he was enjoying being part of it, instead of apart from it.

And then he realized he was staring at *something* in the window of Orchid Jewelers. It was something that made him understand exactly what was happening to him.

Nate Hathoway realized he was falling in love. The exact kind of love Cindy had once wished for him.

The can't-breathe, can't-think, can't-function kind that he had once thought sounded awful.

And Nate realized that if he didn't make a choice about that soon, if he didn't stop *falling,* and start making some conscious decisions, the ability to choose might be taken away from him completely.

He might become helpless in the face of the enormous power of that thing called love.

If there was a word that had not appeared in a Hathoway vocabulary for several centuries, it was that one.

Helpless.

But that's exactly what he felt as he pushed

open the door to the jewelry shop, walked in and went to the counter.

A perky girl in a Santa hat came and smiled at him.

"Can I help you, sir?"

Last chance to break and make a run for it. *Helpless.*

"I'd like to see that ring," Nate said, surprised by how strong his voice was. How absolutely sure. "The one in the window."

He felt a breath on his neck. He whirled and looked around the store. He was the only customer in it.

It must have been the bells in the mall that made him think he had heard Cindy laughing. That made him think he had heard her breathe, *yes.*

Morgan McGuire was not sure she had ever experienced a more perfect or magical night.

The whole town seemed to have gathered at the Old Sawmill Pond for the skating party that welcomed Wesley Wellhaven to Canterbury.

Wesley was the antithesis of his wife. There was no hiding that he was a shy and self-effacing man. His manner was so mild that Morgan wondered if he could really produce the voice he was so famous for.

She voiced that doubt to Nate in a low whisper when they skated off after being introduced to Mr. Wellhaven, who had thanked them both effusively for their hard work on *The Christmas Angel* project.

"It's probably some trickery of the *brains of the outfit,*" Nate said. Despite the miraculous progress Mrs. Wellhaven had made with the children's choir, Nate had never quite forgiven her their initial encounter.

And then they laughed, and Morgan marveled at how easily they laughed together, and how often, and at how the hard lines seemed to be melting from Nate's face, one by one.

"What are you looking at?" he teased.

"You. You're a handsome man, Nate."

"Stop. You'll make me blush." And then he

bent and brushed his lips to hers, and threw back his head and laughed.

Morgan knew it was partly Nate's hand in hers, his easy affection, that made the evening so completely magical. A huge bonfire burned beside the pond, vats of hot chocolate were kept warm, and trays and trays of Christmas cookies sat on tables that had been set up beside the pond.

It was a true community event. Everyone was there, from the mayor to the waitresses, from grandmas and grandpas to small babies being pulled around the ice in sleds.

There were cameras filming some of what would be inserted into the moments right before the commercial breaks of the television special, but after a few minutes of self-consciousness everyone seemed to forget they were there.

But all of this was only a backdrop for what was unfolding inside of her. Nate's hand was always in hers, or his arm around her waist. He would tilt his head to listen to her, or to laugh at something she said.

They were a *couple*, Morgan realized. Everybody knew it. He seemed proud of it and of her.

It came on her suddenly, a delicious sensation of belonging. Not just with him, but in this community.

She did not miss the small smiles people exchanged with them, or the liking and enormous respect these people had for Nate.

She did not miss how much they had hoped for him to be what he was tonight: energized and laughter-filled, mischievous and fun-loving. And because they saw her as part of what was bringing Nate back to them, they accepted her.

Maybe it wasn't even going too far to say that they cared deeply for her, their grade-one teacher, Nate Hathoway's girlfriend.

Girlfriend. She savored the word, like a caramel melting on the tip of her tongue.

Morgan glided across the ice with Nate and a single word formed in her mind. *Belonging.* It was a whisper of something she had waited her whole life to feel.

Morgan had not skated very much, but she soon

found she loved the sensation of gliding along the ice, especially with Nate, a strong skater, beside her.

The children were racing around on their skates, shouting with exuberance, playing games that Ace seemed to always be at the center of.

Nate followed his daughter for a moment with his eyes, then smiled, satisfied. "You've worked a miracle, there, Morgan McGuire," he said. "She's happy. To be truthful? I did not think we could have a happy Christmas ever again."

In the past days, he had told Morgan all about growing up with the Three Musketeers, about the closeness of their friendship, about David and Cindy loving each other so much. And then David going away and not coming back.

He told her how for the longest time he had thought he would lose Cindy, too. She had pined, not eating properly, not going out, the light gone from her eyes. Every day he had gone to her, made her eat, made her get out of the house.

They had become a habit for each other. It

came to a point that he could not imagine life without her.

And he felt they'd had a good marriage. Solid. Based in respect and friendship.

And then Nate told Morgan about the accident that had taken his wife, about that final errand she had gone to run on Christmas Eve and never come back from.

How even in excruciating pain, she had *something* that he could never hope to have. A simple faith. A belief that somehow everything, even this, was unfolding according to a larger plan.

And then Nate told Morgan about his own black days after. There was no one to come rescue him from that feeling of sinking into a mire that he could never get out of. He had told her the worst of it was a sense of having failed.

"A man wants to believe he can protect those he loves from harm. But he can't. Not always. Learning that," Nate had told her, "has been the hardest lesson of my life."

But for a man who had learned hard lessons, he seemed only at ease now as he guided her around the firelit surface of the frozen Old Sawmill Pond. Nate Hathoway seemed only enormously sure of himself and his place in the world.

Morgan wanted the night never to end, but of course, all good things had to end.

As the magical evening drew to a close, Wesley Wellhaven left no doubt about the genuine gift of his magnificent voice.

As far as Morgan knew, what happened next was completely unscripted. Wesley Wellhaven stood by the fire, facing toward all the people skating on the pond, and he began to sing.

No televised concert, no CD could prepare a person for the pureness of his voice in person. It cut through all the chatter, and it soared above the shouts of children. It rose above the skate blades hissing on ice, and climbed above the crackle of the fire.

It inspired silence. The chatter and laughter died. Even a crying baby stopped its caterwauling.

Everyone drifted across the ice to where Wesley stood in front of the fire, his eyes closed, more than his voice pouring out of him.

His spirit. For such a mild man it was so evident his spirit was gigantic.

"His voice must make angels weep," Morgan whispered, and Nate's hand tightened around hers.

It was one of those moments where time stood still, it was a moment that shone with an inner light, that moved with the life force itself.

He sang the oldest of the Christmas songs, but the way he sang it, it was brand-new.

Morgan felt as if she had never heard it before.

Silent night, holy night,
All is calm,
all is bright...

It felt as though Wesley was describing *this* night in its calmness, in its brightness, the hope that was buried in the stillness.

And as he finished, and the people of Canterbury stood in the stillness left by his voice and the winking stars above them, Morgan knew what she felt was more than belonging.

She glanced up at the man who stood beside

her, at the strength in the lines of his face, softened only slightly by the flicker of the fire.

And she knew what she felt was *love*.

Love. Terrifying. Electrifying. Comforting. Calming. It was both breathlessness, and the deepest and most steady breath of all.

Wesley allowed the silence to envelope them, but after a subtle prod in the ribs from his wife's elbow, he cleared his throat, humbly, sweetly uncomfortable being the center of attention.

"And now I have an announcement that many of you have been waiting for," he said. "Mrs. Wellhaven and I have agreed on the child who should sing the final song in the concert, a song called 'Angel of Hope.'"

Morgan knew she was not supposed to hope it was one child above another. And she knew for the one she did hope to be chosen it would take a miracle.

"That child is Brenda Weston."

Though Morgan had known Brenda was likely to be chosen, and though she loved all her children equally, she could not help but feel deflated. Her eyes sought out Cecilia in the crowd.

"Well, I know at least one angel that will be weeping now," Nate said, his voice gruff and hard.

But when Morgan saw Ace, she wasn't weeping. She was hugging her friend with the exuberance of a second-place finalist in a beauty pageant.

"See?" she told Nate. "She's taking it fine."

But Nate was watching his daughter, too, and he said, "If you think she's taking it fine, you don't know the first thing about her."

She looked at his face. Something had hardened in it. She was not sure what, but it made her shiver.

She felt as if he had left something unspoken. *You don't know the first thing about us.*

Morgan was so aware something had shifted ever so slightly, changed. The car ride home was silent, Cecilia exhausted, nearly asleep in her car seat.

Nate dropped Morgan off at her house first.

"No, don't get out," Morgan said, when she saw him opening his door. "Just take Cecilia home and get her to bed. It's a lot of excitement for a little girl."

And a lot of disappointment.

She opened the back door, leaned in and touched Cecilia's arm.

"I'm sorry you weren't chosen as the Christmas Angel, sweetie," she said. "I thought you would have made a wonderful Christmas Angel."

And she meant it. It was too bad the world could not see outside the box. With just the tiniest bit of imagination a child like Cecilia could have easily been the Christmas Angel.

Not that Mrs. Wellhaven had ever looked as if she was burdened with an abundance of imagination.

Cecilia smiled sleepily at Morgan. "But I am going to be the Christmas Angel," she said.

"No, honey," Morgan said carefully, "you're not. Mr. and Mrs. Wellhaven chose Brenda."

"I know it *seems* like they did. But, Mrs.

McGuire, I'm going to be the Christmas Angel. I just know it."

This was announced with such certainty and with such sunny optimism that Morgan was taken aback.

"Stop it," Nate told his daughter sternly. "It's over. And you are not going to be the Christmas Angel."

Cecilia didn't say a word, but she pursed her lips together in a look of stubbornness that at least matched her father's.

And then Nate, not missing the fact Cecilia was not "stopping it" even if she had chosen silence, gave Morgan a dark look that she interpreted as somehow making this her fault. And maybe it was. Should she have better prepared Ace? The girl obviously had had unrealistic hopes that she was now unwilling to let go of, even in the face of evidence it was time to let go.

And maybe it was her fault.

Because as she watched them drive away, it seemed to Morgan she had developed quite a few unrealistic hopes of her own. What had happened to the woman she had been when she had first arrived here in Canterbury?

A woman absolutely committed to leaving her fantasies and fairy tales behind her?

"What happened to her?" she murmured to herself. "The Purple Couch Club can't hold a candle to what I've felt the last few weeks."

But what if she was guilty of passing a silly desire to hope for things that were never going to happen on to the children she taught? They trusted her and treated every single thing she said as gospel, treated every single thing she did as an example of how to live.

In a split second, because of one dark accusing look from Nate, Morgan's night had gone from magic to misery.

And she felt as if she had failed herself.

Because somehow, somewhere, when she'd let her guard down, when she wasn't looking, she'd let herself be swept off her feet.

Morgan McGuire realized the truth. She had fallen in love with Nate Hathoway.

CHAPTER EIGHT

NATE SCANNED the newspaper. And there it was, one more blow for Ace. His name was not among the three hundred names, listed alphabetically, that had received one of those coveted tickets for the rows and rows of uncomfortable chairs he had helped set up in the auditorium. He would not be part of the live audience that got to watch *The Christmas Angel.*

"Buy the newspaper right away, Daddy," Ace had told him when he had dropped her at school. "The names are coming out today. I just know you're going to get one of the tickets, Daddy. I just know it."

It had meant a lot to her that he be there, at *The Christmas Angel,* in person. After her disappointment about not being chosen the angel, he had hoped to at least be able to give her his presence as she sang along with the rest of the angel choir. Especially since his little girl was being such a good sport. It hardly seemed like a glitch on her radar that she hadn't been chosen.

She had just switched her optimism, now it was all focused on Nate getting one of those tickets.

What had it been about her certainty that had almost convinced him that he would get one of the tickets?

He was becoming a dreamer, that's what. Had he actually started to feel, like Ace, as if an angel maybe was watching over them?

Nate, you've been my angel. Now I'll be yours.

It was so unrealistic. So fantasy based, instead of fact based. It could not be a good thing.

His phone rang. He hoped it was Morgan, even though he knew she was teaching school. He hoped it was her, even though he had not called her since the skating party. Holding back. *Proving* to himself he did have control. That he wasn't *helpless*.

The caller was the set designer for *The Christmas Angel*. In a panic. Nate had noticed the people who flooded the town, *The Christmas Angel* production team, were always in a panic about one thing or another.

Today, it had been discovered one of the props wasn't working. A window on the cottage was supposed to slide open, and Mr. Wellhaven was to lean out that window to sing his first song. The window was stuck.

For a minute, the Nate who could already feel his daughter's disappointment that he had not received one of the tickets, wanted to tell the set designer to stuff it. To stuff the whole damn *Christmas Angel*. To stuff himself while he was at it.

But he didn't.

Instead he asked himself, *Where is all this anger coming from?*

Was it because he had bought that damned ring? Or was it because ever since that announcement at the skating party he could feel his hopes dissolving, disappointment circling him and Ace, waiting, like vultures, for the inevitable. As if their very optimism had set them up for the kill.

But he thought of Wesley singing that night at the frozen pond, and he thought of how that voice had eased something in him. Maybe it could do something for the rest of the world when they watched it live.

So, instead of telling the set designer to stuff it, Nate took a deep breath, looked at his watch, said he'd be there as soon as he could to have a look at the window.

He hung up the phone. "Nate saves Christmas," he told himself sarcastically, but even his customary sarcasm felt funny, like a jacket that no longer fit.

No one was on the set or in the auditorium when Nate got there. It was unusual. Usually the whole area bustled with electricians and light people and sound people. But now it was down to the finishing details. Most of the work was done, and Nate had a rare opportunity to stand back and look at what they had accomplished.

It was amazing. The humble school stage had been transformed. It looked like the set for a highly polished and professional production.

The illusion that had been created was nothing short of magical. The cottage, dripping snow, looked amazingly realistic. Suspended snow-flakes that actually moved and changed colors dangled from the ceiling. The tiers the grade-one choir would stand on looked like banks of snow.

And the huge Christmas tree, sent from Canada, a Frasier fir, was stage right. It was filling the whole auditorium with its scent, and it was finally magnificently decorated.

Nate went to the cottage, and went behind it, tested the window. It was sticking. He pulled a screwdriver from his belt, did an adjustment, tried it again. It slid a little more easily, but he wanted it to glide.

The door to the backstage opened and shut, but he paid no attention to the sound of footsteps.

A curtain moved and a shaft of light fell across

him. Nate looked up from where he was crouched below the window, and frowned.

Ace?

What was she doing here by herself? He almost called out a greeting, but some instinct stopped him.

Her intensity, her single-minded focus on *something*.

So instead of calling out a greeting, Nate pulled back into the shadows behind the cottage and stood frozen and silent, watching his daughter tiptoe across the stage.

She went behind the tree, and with the familiarity of someone who had done this a million times, she climbed the staircase, hidden from the audience, that allowed the angel to get to the top of the tree.

Once there, she stood for a moment, radiant. From her lofty height advantage, she smiled out at the empty auditorium.

And then she began to sing.

It was an awful sound, reminiscent of alley cats meeting and greeting under a full moon.

And yet, despite how awful it was, Nate was transfixed.

His daughter looked so beautiful on that perch above the tree, her eyes closed, her arms extended, singing with exuberance that was attractive, even if the tone was not. He recognized the song and realized Ace had been humming and singing that same tune around the house for days.

"Angel of Hope," the number Brenda Weston had been chosen to sing.

As Ace poured her heart into singing now, there was a look on her face that every parent lives to see on the face of their child.

As if she was sure of her place in the world, and was claiming it. And as if she was accepting the world embracing her back.

But for as ethereal as the moment was, Nate realized he could not be transfixed by this! He was her father. And he had to do the responsible thing, even if it hurt. And it was going to hurt, him more than her, not that she ever had to know.

He stepped out from the cottage, stood before the Christmas tree, gazing up at her, his arms folded over his chest.

It took Ace a minute to realize she had an audience. Her eyes opened, her voice faltered and then died. She looked down at him.

"Daddy?"

"Get down from there," he said.

She came down slowly, not demonstrating even half the confidence she had gone up the staircase with. Finally, she stood in front of him, not looking at him, scuffing her toes against the floor.

The backstage door opened again.

"Cecilia?"

The curtain parted again and Morgan stood there, but he held up a hand and focused on his daughter.

"What were you doing?" he asked Ace.

"Just practicing," Ace said in a small voice.

"Practicing what?"

She hesitated. She looked at Morgan for help. Good God, was Morgan in on this?

"Practicing for what?" he said again.

"To be the Christmas Angel," Ace muttered.

"What?"

"I'm going to be the Christmas Angel."

"No, you aren't."

"I am so! I'm going to be the Christmas Angel!" Ace shouted at him.

"Oh, Cecilia," Morgan said, and stepped forward, but he stopped her with a look. It seemed his daughter's ridiculous, impossible, unrealistic hopes only mirrored his own. It felt as if that ring was burning a hole through his shirt pocket.

He didn't need any of what Morgan was bringing to his daughter. Or to him. All that softness and light. And hope.

He'd even started to think, just like his daughter, that an angel was looking after them! It was enough.

False hopes had to be dealt with. And destroyed.

Before they destroyed the one who harbored them.

"You…are…not…going…to…be…the…Christmas…Angel." He enunciated every word carefully. He wanted his daughter to understand how dangerous his mood was.

"I am!" Ace shouted. "I am. My mommy told me I was."

He closed his eyes and asked for the strength to do what needed to be done. "Ace, your mother is dead. She's been dead a long time. She didn't tell you anything."

"She did so! In the dream. She told me! She was an angel."

"There are no angels," he said. He said it firmly, but he could feel something dip inside himself. Who was he to make a statement like that? Still, it felt as though to show his daughter one bit of doubt right now would be the wrong thing. The worst thing.

Tears were coming up in Ace's eyes, furious, hurt, and he knew he couldn't react to them. Or to that funny feeling that he had just said something really, really bad.

For her own good, these hopes had to be dashed.

"Dreams aren't real," he said. "You aren't going

to be the Christmas Angel. Not ever. There's no use thinking it. Brenda Weston is the Christmas Angel."

His daughter looked at him mutinously, not backing down.

"You can't sing," he told her, feeling like Simon in *American Idol*. "You sound awful."

Ace's mouth moved, but for a moment, no sound came out. When it did it was a howl of pain so pure it reminded him of when he had told her Cindy was dead.

He made himself go on. "Brenda looks like the Christmas Angel, and she sounds like the Christmas Angel. She's the perfect Christmas Angel."

"I hate you," Ace screamed, and then ran past him and into Morgan's arms. She buried her head against Morgan, who was looking at him as if he was the devil himself.

"How could you?" she asked quietly.

Yeah, that was the question he was asking himself. How could he have done this? Let hope creep in? Allowed himself and his daughter to

believe impossible things? How could he have
let things go this far?

"It needed to be said." He could hear the grim-
ness in his tone.

"Not like that, it didn't."

"Yeah. It did. Exactly like that."

"You're breaking her heart."

"No," he said quietly. "I'm not. Her heart has
already been broken. Unlike you, I'm doing my
best to make sure it doesn't happen again."

"Unlike me?" Morgan whispered.

"We don't need dreams, Miss McGuire. We
don't need the kind of dreams you represent."

"You're right," she said, her eyes snapping with
indignation and anger. "You don't need dreams.
You need a miracle."

He could tell she was within an inch of stamping her foot and announcing she hated him,
too.

"We don't believe in miracles, either," he said,
his tone deliberately flat, even though he felt that
same little dip in his chest as he said it.

Morgan didn't stamp her foot, or tell him she

hated him. That almost would have been easier to deal with than her look of hurt disdain, of absolute betrayal. She gathered Ace in close to her, and they left the stage.

Only after the door was shut, did Nate allow himself to crumple. He sat on the edge of the stage, and buried his head in his hands.

"Okay," he said. "Okay, if there are angels, or miracles, I could sure use one now."

He felt instantly ridiculous.

And all he felt was that same yawning emptiness he had felt on those pitiful occasions he had gone to Cindy's grave, hoping to feel something. Anything.

It felt as though the darkness was gathering around him, pitch-black, tarlike, so thick and so sticky that nothing, least of all light, would ever penetrate it again.

Morgan looked around her little house. The tree was down. Most of her dishes and clothing were packed in boxes stacked along her living room wall.

The coat hangers remained in the hall. She could not bear to take those with her.

She had, she acknowledged, had a problem her whole life. She cared about everything way too much, way too deeply.

She had fallen in love with Ace Hathoway.

And even more, she had fallen in love with her father.

Over the past few weeks, she had cherished a dream. That they were all going to be together, that they were going to be a family. With each moment spent with Nate, with each time he had held her hand, teased her, looked at her, kissed her, her dreams had billowed to life. Filled her. Made her feel something she had never really felt.

Complete.

How could she stay here, feeling that way, loving them both so much and knowing her dreams, like Ace's own, were not based in reality?

It was just wishful thinking. It was just dreams.

"We don't need dreams, Miss McGuire. We don't need the kind of dreams you represent."

The words had been hurtful enough. The way he had been so harsh with Ace had been devastating. The memory of the look on his face—angry, closed—still had the power to make Morgan shiver.

She'd made a mistake thinking she saw things in him that weren't there. She'd made a mistake of the heart.

She was always making mistakes of the heart.

But the thought of him *knowing* how deeply he'd hurt her was unbearable. She had to get out of here with what little was left of her pride intact.

So, as soon as she got her kids through the production of *The Christmas Angel,* she was going.

On Christmas Day, when everyone was busy with their families, cocooned in those circles of love she had longed for, Morgan would and could just slip away unnoticed. She would get in her little car, the tank already filled with gas, and she would go to anywhere. It didn't matter where. She had some savings. She would leave a check here for January's rent. And then, when she found where she wanted to be, she would hire movers to come get her things.

But maybe she'd tell them to leave the purple sofa.

Maybe she'd just leave everything. Maybe she'd join her mother and they could be blissfully single in Thailand together.

No, her mother was not going to make her happy. And neither was being single.

It was only part of the lies she had spun around herself. The lie that independence could be a suitable replacement for her heart's greatest longing. It was a lie he had shattered at the same time he had no intention of replacing it.

She had seen that in his face.

Morgan had seen something so hard and cold in his face, she knew she could not trespass there.

If only she had paid attention to that sign, the

first day, that said everything she had needed to know about Nate Hathoway.

Go Away.

Now she would. For her own self-preservation she would go away.

What about my kids? She wailed to herself. *How would they find a replacement at this time of year. Who would teach them?*

But then she pulled herself up. She was not thinking one thought that made her weak instead of strong. Not one.

Nate thought, by deciding to not call Morgan ever again, by deciding not to give her that ring, he could manage to cheat grief.

Instead, he found out his acquaintance with grief thus far had only touched the surface of where that emotion could go.

With Cindy and with David, there had been no second chances, no second-guessing, no going back…

He'd been forced to say goodbye.

But Morgan lived. She breathed. Her presence

in his town, just minutes away from him, beckoned and called.

It made him question himself, his decisions, his sanity.

Ace, who normally forgave him everything, was not forgiving him this. Living with her holding a grudge against him was a form of torment he could not have imagined. And yet to back down, what would that mean?

What would it mean in the long run if he encouraged his daughter to believe in impossible dreams?

Gee, Ace, go ahead. Believe you're going to be the Christmas Angel. Believe it right up until the moment it doesn't happen. Go ahead.

It wasn't the responsible thing to do.

Falling for Morgan had not been the responsible thing to do, either.

To add to his sense of grief he was furious at himself. He was in a pit of recrimination and failure.

He thought he had known darkness before. But he had not even touched the surface of that place that was so black it could swallow a man's soul, whole.

Christmas Eve. Ace had been dropped off in her choir angel costume at the school. She had not looked at him, nor kissed him goodbye.

The absence of the words, *I love you, Daddy* made the world he moved in darker.

Molly and Keith had asked him to join them at the community hall to watch the live feed of the concert, but he wasn't going to.

He was going to sit at home, in his darkness, revel in it, relish it.

And that was exactly what he was doing, when his doorbell rang.

And then, when he chose to ignore it, again, and then again.

Finally, when whoever stood out there made it evident they had no intention of giving up, Nate went and answered it ready to let all his bad temper out on an unsuspecting someone.

But he was astonished that it was Wesley Wellhaven standing here.

Wesley was already in the dark tux he would

perform in. He looked wildly uncomfortable. And at the same time, as he had shown by ringing the doorbell over and over again, determined.

"Mr. Hathoway, you need to come." His voice carried urgency. "I have a place for you at the concert."

Nate looked down at the way he was dressed, jeans and a T-shirt. He looked at Mr. Wellhaven's tuxedo. His mouth moved. He tried to say no, he was choosing darkness, but the words wouldn't come out.

"Please don't make me late," Wesley pleaded. "We are live tonight. A foolish idea. I can't tell you how I hate live."

It was apparent to Nate that Wesley Wellhaven, for some reason known only to himself, was prepared to keep the whole world waiting while he talked Nate into coming to his production.

He remembered already thinking, once this week, he could not deprive the world of the gift of this man's voice.

With a sigh, he grabbed his jacket out of the coat closet and allowed Wesley to guide him down to where a long stretch limo waited at the end of his walk.

Once in the limo, Wesley ducked his head, fiddled with his bow tie, glanced at Nate. "I have a confession to make."

"To me?" Nate said. This must be some kind of case of mistaken identity.

"Yes, to you, Mr. Hathoway. I was there."

"Excuse me?"

"I was there. When you argued with your daughter. I like to sit in the seats of the empty auditorium before a performance. I like to see the stage as the poorest audience member will see it. And then make changes to try and make their experience more enjoyable.

"And so, I am embarrassed to say, I saw your very private moment with your daughter."

"Oh," Nate said. "I think it's me who should be embarrassed."

The limo pulled up to the school. Wesley pressed a ticket into Nate's hand.

"Yes, indeed you should at least share the embarrassment, Mr. Hathoway. How could you tell your daughter there is no such thing as a miracle? Why, they happen all the time."

"With all due respect, Mr. Wellhaven, no they don't."

"Really? Then see if you can explain how a humble and mild man such as myself was given such a voice," he challenged. He waited. Nate did not have an answer to that. "Enjoy the performance, Mr. Hathoway. And have faith. If you teach your daughter nothing else, teach her to believe in miracles."

And then he was gone.

And Nate looked at the ticket in his hands, and knew he had no choice but to go in. Or walk home.

But that day, sitting on the stage, his head in his hands, he'd asked for a miracle. What if this was it?

Oh, sure, Hath, he chided himself. *Believe one last time.* But the truth was he could not have prevented himself from going into that auditorium.

Of course he was the last one in there, and

had to shove his way past all the people already seated to what seemed to be the only remaining chair in the whole place.

And of course, it had to be right beside her.

Morgan McGuire gave him her snippiest look. And when he scraped back his chair, she placed a finger to pursed lips.

"Shh," she said sternly.

He wondered if she could hear the beating of his heart. To be so near to her, the one he had told himself he could never have, was a form of the purest torture he had ever experienced.

Then the lights went down, and the children's choir filed onto the stage. He noticed immediately Ace was not among them.

Morgan turned to him. "Where is she?" she whispered, real concern replacing her snippiness.

Nate's heart began to race in fear. He thought of the cold war at home. And her disappointments.

Where was his daughter?

And then, just when he thought he would get

up and tear the building apart to look for Ace, he saw the curtain open a tiny crack, and Ace peered out at the crowd, then at the choir.

"There she is," he whispered to Morgan.

"But what is she doing?"

Ace was looking woefully at the children's choir. She dropped the curtain again.

But not before he had seen the look on her face when she had seen Brenda, who now stood in the choir angel costume with the rest of the choir. He looked at Brenda, too. Her normally lovely face was blotchy from crying.

Oh, God. What had Wesley Wellhaven done? As well-meaning as it was, Nate could sense disaster coming.

His sense of it was so strong he could barely enjoy the production despite how good the children's choir had become, despite how amazingly Wesley blended his voice with those of the children. Despite the fact the evening was an inspiration and a gift to the world, just as Nate had hoped, he could not relax. And he could not enjoy it.

Morgan seemed equally tense beside him.

Finally, they reached the last number. The lights in the whole building went out, and only one came back on.

It was true.

His daughter was the Christmas Angel. There she was on her perch above the Christmas tree, all the lights now turned off except the one brilliantly white spotlight that was on her.

That familiar music started, and he felt himself cringing waiting for her to begin singing.

But Ace didn't start to sing.

On cue, she began to speak the role that had been a singing one. Her voice, despite the croakiness of it, was loud and strong.

Then it wobbled.

She picked up, but then it wobbled again.

And then Nate's little Christmas Angel, on live television, in front of the whole world, started crying.

And then she stopped, and in a voice that had absolutely no croak to it, that was strong and sure and beautiful, Ace Hathoway said, "If for one person to be happy, another has to be sad, that's wrong. And it's not Christmas. Brenda, you come be the Christmas Angel."

And with grave dignity, she turned around and went down the stairs at the back of the tree, pulled back the heavy velvet curtain and slipped through it.

Nate got up out of his seat. And somehow his hand was in Morgan's and he was taking her with him.

As Brenda quickly made her way up the steps to the top of the tree, Nate and Morgan slipped backstage.

"How could you, you little wretch?" Mrs. Wellhaven had Ace's shoulders in her bony fingers and was snarling at her.

"Take your hands off my daughter before I bean you," Nate said.

Mrs. Wellhaven turned and gave him a look that could have slayed dragons. But he went right by her and scooped up his daughter in his arms.

Ace's tears flowed down his neck.

"I ruined it, didn't I, Daddy? I ruined *The Christmas Angel?*"

He could hear Brenda's sweet voice filling the auditorium.

"No, sweetheart, you didn't. You made me really proud. That was a good, good thing to do. The kind of thing only someone with a good heart would think of."

"I didn't wreck it?"

"No. I think you made it the best Christmas show, ever."

He and Morgan and Ace stood there, in the back of the stage, Ace's tears sliding down his neck as Brenda sang the song, and then Wesley's powerful voice joined hers as they sang the final number together.

In a moment, as the voices faded, thunderous applause filled the auditorium.

And when it died completely, someone out there yelled, "We want the redheaded angel."

It was a small town, and someone else provided her name.

"We want Ace. We want Ace Hathoway," a man called out.

Now it was like thunder, a chant that was picked up and called out. "We want Ace. We want Ace. We want Ace."

When it could not be ignored a moment longer, when it felt as if the very roof would fall in under the tremendous volume of that demand, Morgan tugged at his sleeve and ducked under the curtain, bringing him with her.

He looked out at the sea of faces. He saw his friends and his neighbors. And he saw they were on their feet, whistling and stamping.

And he got it.

These people saw Ace's spirit, her willingness to give even though it hurt her, her willingness to put another's well-being ahead of her own.

He remembered her words the night after she had had the dream.

Ace had told him her mommy was going to save Christmas. That her mommy was going to show people what it was really all about.

And he could see that's exactly what had

happened. He saw the true spirit of Christmas in his daughter's generous spirit. In the people cheering for her. In Wesley Wellhaven's brave, brave choice to choose a less than perfect Christmas Angel.

And he saw it in Morgan, in the way she was looking at them both, with such love, smiling through her tears.

And the Light broke apart the darkness and chased it from him, like the sun chasing away the last of the storm.

His daughter had just taught him something that was not just a lesson for Christmas, but a lesson for life.

Love gave. Love didn't ask what it was getting back. Love didn't say, *you might hurt me, so I'm not going to try at all.*

Love said, *give everything you've got, every single minute that you've got it.* Love said, *time is short. Don't waste one precious moment of it being afraid, or protecting yourself.*

Love said, *risk all. It's worth it to know Me.*

And in that moment of illumination, Nate knew Wesley was right. And so was Morgan.

Miracles did happen. They came in the form of people, and insights and moments of inspiration. They came on the magnificent voice of a humble man, and the humble voice of a magnificent girl.

Wasn't that what Christmas did? Reminded people, all over again, especially the weary, especially those who had forgotten, especially those who felt downtrodden, especially those who felt beaten, to hope for a miracle. And to believe it would come.

But a person had to be open to that miracle coming. He had to be willing to see.

Or they would slip away if they were not acknowledged. And maybe after a while, if a man turned his back on enough miracles, maybe they wouldn't come back anymore at all.

As if to show how easily things could slip away, Morgan moved away from him and Ace, and over to her first graders. She was instantly surrounded in their clamor. Even from here he could here them calling for her attention.

"Mrs. McGuire. Mrs. McGuire."

She went down on her knees and opened her arms. In a moment he could not see her for all the wriggling bodies trying to get close to her, to hug her, to cuddle with her.

A man could make his own darkness. And he could live in it forever.

But Nate Hathoway wasn't going to. Not anymore.

What seemed to be a long time ago, Morgan had told him she was going to spend Christmas alone.

And he had known she wasn't.

Now he knew she wasn't ever going to again. Not as long as she lived and breathed. Not as long as he lived and breathed.

If she said yes.

Standing there on that stage, with his daughter in his arms and the woman he loved with that head-over-heels kind of love that made it impossible for a man to breathe or think or function, with the whole town on their feet whistling and clapping, he felt a breath on his neck.

And heard her whisper, once, *yes*.

He glanced at Morgan and realized she had not said a word.

And he realized, his heart swelling, that he and his daughter and the woman he loved stood among angels.

Morgan looked around her tiny house sadly. She snapped her tiny suitcase shut, put her book *Bliss: The Extraordinary Joy of Being a Single Woman* on top of it.

She was going to cry. She knew it.

Just thinking of those last moments on stage— not Ace's performance, or Brenda's, either—but the moment those children had surrounded her. She had hugged each and every one, only she knowing the truth.

Goodbye.

When she thought of not seeing her kids again, or her friends at the school, when she thought of not seeing Nate and Ace, the lump in her throat grew so large she could not even swallow.

Of course, she was going to cry for the rest of her life every single time she thought of Ace, *The Christmas Angel,* giving up her dream so that her friend could have hers.

She was going to cry for the rest of her life every single time she thought of these days before Christmas that she had spent with Nate.

They had a shine to them that was imprinted on her soul.

She was exhausted. She should probably wait for morning, but the thought of waking up alone on Christmas morning in this sweet little house was more than she could bear.

Just as she moved toward the door, there was a tap on it. Morgan froze, thinking she might have imagined it, thinking that maybe a branch had tapped the window.

But no, there it came again.

She tiptoed to her front window, craned her neck and could see her doorstep. Nate stood there.

Now what?

She was determined to go, to give this independent life a genuine shot. To make it a success this time. To not be swept from her chosen path.

He had gotten in the way before, a test that she had failed.

Maybe he was still testing her. And she wasn't going to fail this time.

Hoping only she would ever know her boldness was a complete pretext, she went and threw open the door.

"Hi."

"Nate."

His eyes drank her in, like a man who had crossed the desert, and she was a long cool drink of water.

Then his eyes left her, found the suitcase, went back to her. He frowned.

"Did you decide to go spend Christmas with your family after all?"

"Yes," she lied. So much easier than saying, *I am running away from you who wants no part of me or the kind of dreams I offer.*

Something in her voice tipped him off, because his eyes went back to her face, suddenly skeptical. Without being invited, he moved by her and stood in her living room.

"What happened to your tree?"

"I took it down. I didn't want to come home—" her voice caught on the word *home,* but she rushed on "—to find a pile of needles on the floor."

He was looking now at the boxes packed neatly on top of the purple couch. His eyes scanned her living room.

"Where's all the highly breakable bric-a-brac?" he asked.

She said nothing.

"Are you leaving?"

She couldn't look at him. Her shoulders were shaking. She looked down at her feet. She was mortified to see a teardrop on the end of her shoe.

His feet moved into her line of vision. One lean finger came under her chin and lifted it.

"You can't leave," he said huskily. "We've just begun."

But it was him who wasn't leaving. He took off his jacket and hung it on one of *their* coat hangers. He set down a wrapped Christmas package beside it.

"You said you didn't need me or my kind of dreams," she reminded him shakily, as he turned back to her and regarded her with those steady eyes.

We've just begun? That weakness was sweeping her, that *longing* was knocking the legs right out from under her.

She pulled away from him, caught a glance of her book sitting on top of her luggage, a stern reminder of the bliss that awaited her if she could just get through this.

"Did you know," she told him, "whole cultures are dispensing with relationships?"

He folded his arms over the mightiness of his chest, she suspected to keep himself from shaking her, but she bravely went on.

"In some Scandinavian countries, Denmark,

Iceland, women are *choosing* not to get married anymore. They still have children, they've just dispensed with the, er, bothersome part."

"You mean men?" he asked grimly.

"Yes," she said, tilting her chin at him, "the bothersome part."

"Ah. The insensitive part."

"Uh-huh."

"The part that tends to run and hide when something like commitment begins to look likely."

"Exactly."

"The part that looks for an excuse to drive people away when they start getting too close."

Was he talking about *him* or about her? Because wasn't that what she was doing? Literally driving away because she had gotten too close. Her relationship with Karl had never asked this much of her, but she had driven away from that one, too.

"Well, dispensing with men is probably all well and good, we are a bothersome lot, but who puts up their coat hangers?"

"I'm sure they hire it out."

"Ditto for Christmas trees?"

"I haven't got to that part of the book, yet."

"And who deals with the stubborn ponies?"

"Not everyone has a stubborn pony to deal with."

"Who do they teach to make cookies?"

"Their children."

"Ah, the children that they dispensed with the bother of giving a father. How do the children feel about that?"

"I don't know," she said, a little querulously. "I don't know any Scandinavian children. Or Scandinavian women for that matter."

He moved closer to her, stared down at her.

"Who holds them in the night, Morgan? Who do they laugh with? Who do they hold hands with? Who do they kiss? Who makes the loneliness go away? Who makes the sun come out when it's raining?"

"You can't make the sun come out when it's raining!" Oh, hell. They weren't even talking about him. They were talking in *general* terms. Why had she said that?

But he moved closer to her. "Try me," he breathed.

"It's not raining."

"It is in my world, Morgan. The thought of you going away is making it rain in my world."

And then he closed the small distance between them, bent, cupped his hand at the back of her neck and drew her lips to his.

She willed herself to pull away in the interests of being the woman she should be.

But it seemed when her lips met his, she discovered, anew, exactly who that was.

"It's working for me," he said softly against her lips. "The sun is coming out for me, Morgan. And I know. Because I've been without it for a long time. Do you have to go there? Do you have to see for yourself what a lonely place the world can be?"

His lips took hers again before she could answer.

"I've been married," he said to her, a whisper.

"And I've been single. A good marriage is the best, Morgan. You live with your best friend. You aren't lonely anymore."

She could feel something stilling in her, rising up to meet him.

"And you know what else, Morgan? You don't have to be afraid."

And that said it all. All her life she had thought she was afraid her dreams would not come true.

Now, she could see, she was much more afraid they would. What could ever live up to the expectation she had in her mind, after all? How long before the disillusionment set in? How long before one of them crashed out the door in the middle of the night and never came back?

Stunned, she realized she was repeating the pattern of her childhood. She was abandoning the ship because of exactly what he had just said.

Morgan was afraid.

He looked at her, and in his eyes, she knew he

could see her fear. He took her hand, and guided it gently to his face.

And found what he had said was true.

She did not have to be afraid anymore.

She touched his face with her fingertips, explored it. The word *beloved* came to her mind and stayed.

"Don't go, Morgan. Stay. Stay and marry me. I love you. I have loved you from the first moment you ignored my Go Away sign."

"You didn't. You were annoyed by me."

"Some part of me may have been annoyed. Another part knew that you had come to get me. To pull me out of the darkness. And now, I'm coming to get you, Morgan. I don't care what they do in Iceland. I don't want you to be alone."

She could hardly believe what she had just heard, what he had just offered, but when she saw his face, she knew it was true.

"Look," he said. "I got you a Christmas present."

He handed her the package he had set on the floor.

"This is one of the worst wrapping jobs I've ever seen," she said, tears, this time of joy, sparking in her eyes.

"You have a lifetime to teach me how to wrap parcels. And bake cookies."

The wrapping fell away, and she saw the hammer he had picked for her. And tied to its sturdy handle with a fine piece of gold wire was a ring.

"And I have a lifetime to show you," he continued softly, "how to hang coat hangers and choose the right hammer. I have all kinds of skills you don't know about, too."

She could feel herself blushing, and he grinned wickedly.

"Well, there is that. But I'm also a champion diaper changer. You don't get that in every man."

And that the miracle she had waited her whole life for had just come. To have someone to lean on. To belong. To love.

"Will you?" he asked softly. "Will you come and spend Christmas Eve out at Molly and Keith's? And spend Christmas Day with us?"

"Yes," she whispered.

"We'll start there, then," he decided. He took the hammer from her, carefully unwound the sparkling diamond ring and slid it onto her finger.

She held up her hand, and the ring twinkled, and diamond sparks of light flew from it.

That matched the sparks of light that flew from his eyes.

"Yes," Morgan whispered again. Not just to Christmas Eve and Christmas Day, but to a life spent beside this man, bathed in the Light.

EPILOGUE

THE GRAVEYARD WAS QUIET and cold, a little daylight lingered in a cobalt-blue sky. The deep snow muffled his footprints. It was not where everyone would spend a Christmas Eve, but Nate had been drawn here tonight.

"I hope not to escape my mother-in-law," he muttered wryly.

But, of course, it was partly to escape her. Morgan's mother, who used to be plain old Anne, but had changed her name to Chosita after her long stay in Thailand. She said she had adopted the new moniker because everyone had called her that there. She said it meant happiness.

Morgan elbowed Nate in the ribs hard, when he said, coincidentally they had a pony by the same name and that he had almost exactly the same disposition. Nate had since found out that Chosita could indeed mean happiness, but it was sort of the American equivalent of "Hey, lady!"

Morgan's mother drove him nuts, wearing her Thai sarongs in downtown Canterbury where she improved stocks in the bookstore by adding to her substantial self-help collection.

But Ace adored her, and Morgan was thrilled that her mother was here to spend Christmas with them. Morgan genuinely hoped the baby, due any day, would put in an appearance while her mom was here.

Nate exacted subtle revenge on Chosita for what he saw as her astoundingly poor parenting throughout Morgan's childhood and adolescence. This afternoon, for instance, he subjected her to the longest sleigh ride in Happy history. He'd made sure to ply her with several buckets of tea first, too.

He smiled, now, just thinking of it, then knelt beside the two stones.

He knew flowers couldn't handle the cold, so he always brought sprigs of holly, and a fir bough with a candle in it that he would light before he left, and that would burn through to Christmas morning.

"I know, I know," he said, as he brushed the snow from the two stones, "I'm being uncharitable for Christmas. It's just her, really."

The wind howled.

"Okay, so I've never warmed to Mrs. Wellhaven, either."

He had just gotten a thank-you note from the Wellhavens for the intricate iron fireplace grate he had sent them. He never forgot Wesley, or the debt he felt he owed to the man who had not left him in the darkness that Christmas Eve two years ago.

As it had turned out, the whole economy of Canterbury had not been saved by the production of *The Christmas Angel,* but it had certainly been helped over the hump.

As it had turned out, the second annual Christmas production had been the last one Wesley gave.

Shortly after *The Christmas Angel,* Wesley had gone back into retirement to lead the quiet reclusive life he enjoyed. There had been no more Christmas productions, and people thought he did not sing at all. Every now and then one of the tabloids would run a story about the tragic loss of his voice.

But of course Nate knew that not to be true, because on the finest day of his life, when he had stood at the altar waiting for the woman who would be his wife to come toward him, *that* voice had filled the cathedral. Between the beauty of that voice and the beauty of his bride, there had not been a dry eye in the house that afternoon, including his own.

And so, every year, he sent the Wellhavens something.

His reputation as a tough guy seemed to have largely gone out the window as he courted Morgan, anyway. The whole town had seen he was smitten. And he didn't care.

He had serenaded her. He'd delivered wagons of flowers pulled by a reluctant Happy. He had taken her on picnics, and sat at home in front of the fire with her.

Cindy would have been proud. He had not wasted one minute, not one, of that glorious falling-in-love feeling that she had wished for him. He still didn't. He didn't think a man should ever take the gifts he had been given for granted.

Ace was eight now. She was in hockey *and* ballet. She also, much to Happy's distress (the pony, not her grandmother) had started taking riding lessons at the stable where Brenda Weston rode.

The instructor had suggested Ace was ready for a better horse, but Ace had said no. In a statement reminiscent of her famous *Christmas Angel* production speech, she said that if being a good rider meant leaving Happy behind, she would just stay where she was, thanks.

Ace's little speech that had gone live all over North America, was played as one of that year's highlights on almost every news station in America. It was still, two years later, one of the most popular hits on the Internet.

Ace was still tickled when a piece of fan mail reached her.

As far as Nate knew, Brenda, the one everyone, including him, had proclaimed to be the perfect Christmas Angel, had never gotten a single piece of fan mail. But then Brenda, nice as she was, just didn't have the heart Ace had. When the riding instructor had suggested she trade up to a better horse, she'd gotten rid of her epileptic Welsh pony, O'Henry, without a backward glance.

"Which means," he finished softly, "I'm now feeding two ponies, and have double trouble when I try to harness them to the sleigh. At least O'Henry doesn't bite. Okay, he falls over now and then, but who asked for a perfect life?"

He realized he had spoken each of his thoughts out loud, and he smiled. Once, all he had felt here was yawning emptiness.

Now when he came, he felt *full*.

He finished dusting the snow off each of the stones, and then he put the holly and the fir bough between them.

He read them, out loud, too.

David Henderson, gone with angels, son, friend, soldier.

Cynthia Dawn Hathoway. Beloved wife and mother.

When he had chosen this plot next to David, he had known that though Cindy had married him she had really belonged with David. Heart and soul. Forever. That is who she had been crazy in love with since she was fourteen years old.

Still, she had been beloved to Nate. And she had become his Christmas angel. There was not a doubt in his mind that somehow, in some way, in ways that were far too huge for the human mind to grapple with, she had been there that Christmas he had found Morgan.

Bringing meaning out of tragedy. Showing him she had been right all along. Everything had a reason. And good could come from bad.

Somehow Cindy had a hand in bringing him and Ace the woman who would be the best mom for her daughter.

And the best wife for him.

My wish for you is that you could fall in love.

"I did," Nate said out loud. "I have. Crazy in love, just like you always wanted. It's better than anything I could have ever imagined."

Right now, Morgan and Ace and Grandma Happiness were at home making Christmas cookies and decorating the tree he had put the lights on earlier. He had warned Morgan, direly, about getting on the ladder to put up the higher decorations. Naturally, she had stuck out her tongue at him, which meant she was probably on the top rung of the ladder—the one that said "do not use this as a step"—right now.

The baby was due in the first part of the New Year. Ace was more excited about that than she was about Christmas.

They had chosen not to find out the sex. A boy or a girl, either would be a blessing.

Nate lit the candle. It was getting dark and that candle was a small light in that darkness, but a small light could be enough.

He knew Cindy wasn't really here. Nor was

David. He knew love didn't go into the ground. It went on and on. It lived in the people left behind.

Still, he needed to come here, even if they were not here. He needed to come here to remind himself to be grateful for things he could not understand. Angels.

Miracles.

Especially Christmas ones.

"Thank you," he said softly.

Yes. He heard it as clearly as though they stood on either side of him. Exuberant. Triumphant.

That word, that simple affirmation of love and of life, was so real that Nate glanced over his left shoulder, and then his right one. The graveyard was empty. He was alone.

But not really. Not ever.

He was not alone. And he was full. To the top. And then to overflowing.

MILLS & BOON PUBLISH EIGHT LARGE PRINT TITLES A MONTH. THESE ARE THE TITLES FOR APRIL 2011.

———————————————— ❧ ————————————————

NAIVE BRIDE, DEFIANT WIFE
Lynne Graham

NICOLO: THE POWERFUL SICILIAN
Sandra Marton

STRANDED, SEDUCED...PREGNANT
Kim Lawrence

SHOCK: ONE-NIGHT HEIR
Melanie Milburne

MISTLETOE AND THE LOST STILETTO
Liz Fielding

ANGEL OF SMOKY HOLLOW
Barbara McMahon

CHRISTMAS AT CANDLEBARK FARM
Michelle Douglas

RESCUED BY HIS CHRISTMAS ANGEL
Cara Colter

**MILLS & BOON PUBLISH EIGHT
LARGE PRINT TITLES A MONTH.
THESE ARE THE TITLES FOR MAY 2011.**

━━━━━━━━━━━ ❧ ━━━━━━━━━━━

HIDDEN MISTRESS, PUBLIC WIFE
Emma Darcy

JORDAN ST CLAIRE:
DARK AND DANGEROUS
Carole Mortimer

THE FORBIDDEN INNOCENT
Sharon Kendrick

BOUND TO THE GREEK
Kate Hewitt

WEALTHY AUSTRALIAN, SECRET SON
Margaret Way

A WINTER PROPOSAL
Lucy Gordon

HIS DIAMOND BRIDE
Lucy Gordon

JUGGLING BRIEFCASE & BABY
Jessica Hart

Discover Pure Reading Pleasure with

Visit the Mills & Boon website for all the latest in romance

 Buy all the latest releases, backlist and eBooks

 Find out more about our authors and their books

 Join our community and chat to authors and other readers

 Free online reads from your favourite authors

 Win with our fantastic online competitions

 Sign up for our free monthly eNewsletter

 Tell us what you think by signing up to our reader panel

 Rate and review books with our star system

www.millsandboon.co.uk

 Follow us at twitter.com/millsandboonuk

Become a fan at facebook.com/romancehq

ML

4
/11